What the critics say:

Ms. Ballou draws this story with perfect finesse... great characters... Pete is written as an unlikely male character... Lily is a modern independent woman written with great detail... Get out all the toys... This is a highly entertaining book with a great sense of humor and a few twists thrown in to make it more than a typical erotic romance." - *Just Erotic Romance Reviews*

Once again, Ms. Ballou has written a story with enchanting characters who are well developed and are sure to entertain. The distinctive story line will grasp the reader's imagination and give one several hours of gratifying pleasure... characters that will pull at your heart. They are intelligent, strong, and very realistic in nature... the sparks fly from combustible heat. With the abundant, keen humor making this reader laugh out loud, this story will definitely keep you amused, and I was sorry to see it end." - *eCataRomance Reviews*

"This book had me laughing out loud at the twists and turns... a wonderful and delightful tale... Following in the footsteps of its predecessor, this book is a fun sequel." - *The Romance Studio*

"For Pete's Sake is a story of revenge, ambition, and the sensual adventures of a couple who do not appear likable at first glance... an erotic story with a humor-filled plot... Mardi Ballou knows how to raise the heat in her writing, and has penned a tale that is sure to please. Crank up the air conditioning... you will need it" - *Romance Reviews Today*

ELLORA'S CAVE
ROMANTICA PUBLISHING

Discover for yourself why readers can't get enough of the multiple award-winning publisher Ellora's Cave. Whether you prefer e-books or paperbacks, be sure to visit EC on the web at www.ellorascave.com for an erotic reading experience that will leave you breathless.

www.ellorascave.com

FOR PETE'S SAKE
An Ellora's Cave Publication, November 2004

Ellora's Cave Publishing, Inc.
PO Box 787
Hudson, OH 44236-0787

ISBN #1-4199-5083-5

ISBN MS Reader (LIT) ISBN # 1-84360-857-X
Other available formats (no ISBNs are assigned):
Adobe (PDF), Rocketbook (RB), Mobipocket (PRC) & HTML

FOR PETE'S SAKE © 2004 MARDI BALLOU

ALL RIGHTS RESERVED. This book may not be reproduced in whole or in part without permission.

This book is a work of fiction and any resemblance to persons, living or dead, or places, events or locales is purely coincidental. They are productions of the authors' imagination and used fictitiously.

Edited by *Raelene Gorlinsky*
Cover art by *Darrell King*

FOR PETE'S SAKE:
PANTASIA

MARDI BALLOU

Chapter One

"Be finished soon?" the custodian asked, turning on his vacuum cleaner. Pete Payne, startled by the machine's drone suddenly breaking the room's silence, looked up bleary-eyed at the man. They were the only ones still working at this hour of the night at the San Diego office of Fantasia Resorts, Inc.

"Just about done," Pete said, more to himself than the custodian, glancing at his Mickey Mouse watch and registering how really late it was. "Give me a minute, and I'll get out of your way." The man grunted and continued vacuuming.

Pete keyed in the final strokes to complete his project, logged off his computer, and cleared his desk with a satisfied sigh. Revenge, after all, was sweet. It was now late Tuesday night, Pacific time. By this time tomorrow, he'd be in Miami, en route to the Isla del Oro in the Caribbean. And on this coming Saturday, he'd watch the results of his scheme as an uninvited guest at the wedding of Gwyn Verde, his former almost-fiancée, and Dominic Laredo, the billionaire playboy, his soon-to-be-ex-boss. At the moment, Pete was the only person in the universe who knew the wedding was about to turn from an A-list social event to a black eye for Laredo.

Pete drove to a buddy's garage, where he'd stow his car while he was away. His friend, one of the "Lost Boys" he hung out with, would drive him to the airport in the morning. Still keyed up, Pete walked the mile and a half home from his friend's house. The quiet of the dark streets did little to calm him. He scrounged in his kitchen, munched the few remaining chips in the solitary bag lurking on top of the empty fridge, then hopped into the shower for a quick clean-up. As he dragged the comb through his too-long brown hair, he wondered if he should have gotten a haircut. His blue eyes red-rimmed with fatigue, he knew he had to get some decent sleep before he'd next see Gwyn.

After packing his duffel bag and laptop for the plane, Pete tried to settle down for the night. But sleep eluded him. As he began to think about seeing Gwyn in less than three days, Pete's smoldering resentment gave way to a tightening in his groin. He and Gwyn had been so good together. Without her in his life, he was experiencing new and unwelcome levels of horniness. Pete absentmindedly touched his burgeoning erection and closed his eyes.

There'd been no woman in his life since Gwyn had taken off with Dominic Laredo last fall. Here it was spring, when a young man's fancy and all that... And still no woman around except Griselda... Griselda, the semi-anatomically correct life-size inflatable doll his buddies had bought as a gag gift when Gwyn dumped him for Laredo. Some gag. These late nights, Griselda was beginning to look real good to him. Too good. He kept her sprawled on the chair next to his bed, on top of computer magazines, comic books, catalogs, and several Sunday sports pages.

Before Gwyn left him, it had been years since Pete had resorted to whacking off to relieve his tension. Now he spent so much time up close and personal with his right hand, he'd probably get the Gold Medal if jerking off ever became an Olympic event. Before Gwyn, he'd always found it easy to have girlfriends. Before Gwyn, he'd never let relationships become too complicated. Hell, he now realized he'd never really been involved in anything that could be called a relationship. Mutual satisfaction and uncomplicated good times—that's what he was all about. Pete winced, remembering Gwyn's complaints. Before she actually left, he'd always felt he had all the time in the world to make things right with her. She'd get over whatever bugged her. Instead, she got over him. His erection began to wilt—but by now, he was committed to going all the way with it. If he didn't come now, a middle of the night hard-on would sabotage any sleep he managed to get.

All he had to do was visualize Gwyn's luscious body spread out on his bed to get hard again. He didn't want to lose his momentum, so he increased the speed and intensity of his strokes. Jerking off was such a simple exercise—especially compared with the hard work of a relationship with a woman like Gwyn. But even now, as he pulled and prodded and stroked and stretched himself in all the right spots, he had to admit his hand came in a poor second.

At first, when Pete finally accepted that Gwyn was really gone, he wanted to resign from his job as a programmer for Laredo's Fantasia Resorts, Inc. But then he decided to bide his time. Because more than anything else, he wanted revenge on Dominic and a chance to win Gwyn back. So he continued to work at Fantasia, actually got accolades for his extra efforts, waiting for his shot at payback. And it came, faster then he'd ever anticipated.

Speaking of coming, Pete was really close to the edge. Imagining himself with Gwyn now, he squeezed harder and stroked faster—and then he thought about her upcoming wedding and lost the orgasmic spark. He groaned. Instead of the relief of a climax, he remained rock-hard and was starting to feel sore from all the frustrated friction.

Damn. Once Pete made Laredo look like a total fool in public, Gwyn would have to admit Pete was the better man after all. Pete couldn't get the vision of a supplicant, repentant Gwyn out of his mind. There she'd be, her gorgeous blonde hair sweeping over her face as she begged him to take her back.

Even that vision wasn't getting him off. Pete was about to reach for his *Victoria's Secret* catalog when Griselda, gleaming in the moonlight coming in the window, caught his eye. Griselda. Pete groaned, remembering the doll was semi-anatomically correct. He wasn't exactly sure what that meant, but it was beginning to sound amazingly…attractive.

Desperate, he reached over and pulled her into the bed, causing a mini-avalanche of the printed matter she'd been balanced on to spill onto the floor. Griselda's facial features included bright blue eyes and blood-red lips, wide open in a big O of surprise. Griselda, already obligingly nude, had large, albeit nippleless, breasts and a hairless triangle at the junction of her solid thighs. Pete ran his fingers over her bubble-gum pink plastic chest and his cock began to throb. If he squeezed her just right, Griselda expressed her one word vocabulary, which sounded like a cross between a groan and a fart. Music to his ears.

Pete lay down on his side and arranged Griselda to face him. "Come here often?" he asked, almost startled by the sound of his own voice in the darkness. When Griselda didn't answer, he squeezed her and interpreted her squeal to be a *yes*. He squeezed her several more times, and her syllable began to even more convincingly resemble a *yes*. He gently opened her legs and, with her *yesses* ringing in his ears, ran his cock along her mound. Alas, though her anatomy did include a hole there, its rough edges snagged at him like thorns from an aggressive rose. But her cool plastic exterior refreshed and excited his overheated penis, so he began to move his hips and hers to create a satisfying friction. Unfortunately, every time Pete thrust hard, Griselda's legs flew open, breaking their contact.

After several moments with Griselda's arms and legs flailing around and her limited conversation now more closely reminding him of excess gas than anything else, Pete's frustration began to rise almost as high as his erection. He grabbed her, hard, and turned her over. Pete discovered that Griselda's cheeks were more welcoming than her pussy triangle. Her maker must have been a butt man. Her buns were tight and full, and the crevice between them deep. Quick investigation by his fingers revealed a small smooth hole. That and the crack between her buns had Pete twitching with the expectation of relief.

He positioned Griselda on her stomach and lay down on top of her, which had her farting loudly in either protest or delight. After several moments of manipulation and experimentation, Pete found the perfect angle for approach. "Here I come, Griselda," he announced. This time when he thrust, Griselda stayed put. Well, hell, a little movement on her part would be welcome. Of course, Griselda being Griselda, Pete had to move her as well as himself. Which was okay. Within moments, Pete had fallen into a rhythm that had him tingling in anticipation. He'd never actually butt-fucked any woman, but now he began to wonder how it would be. Of course not every woman would be as agreeable to doing it as Griselda, but maybe the next time he was with a real woman he'd...

Griselda gave off a huge fart of excitement and Pete felt himself tighten as his body finally geared up for release. At least with Griselda, he didn't have to worry about a condom or having to use the "L" word... If only he could bring her to life, a plastic female Pinocchio... Pete ejaculated into and all over Griselda's buns and sighed with relief. Then he pushed her aside. Oh yeah, things were much simpler with this doll than with a real woman. And for the moment, that had some appeal. But Pete knew dolls like Griselda had a limited future as playmates. If he thrust too hard or dug his nails into her, he'd probably puncture her and she'd fly the hell off, probably get stuck on his ceiling. He needed a woman. He again toyed with the thought that Gwyn would come back to him. She'd always complained he treated her as thoughtlessly... Maybe like a plastic doll... Had he?

Pete tissued the cum off himself and his partner. "Thanks, honey," he said to her, not quite able to bring himself to kiss her but grateful all the same. "Thanks, guys," he added, sending a message to his buddies. At last his eyelids fluttered and sleep began to claim him.

* * * * *

In the executive cottage that was one the perks of her job, Lily Tiger, manager of Fantasia Resorts' Isla de Oro Caribbean resort, was pacing the length of her bedroom. On this glorious moonlit Tuesday night, the sounds of the sea lapping up on the nearby beach would have lulled most people into sweet dreams. But Lily Tiger had not gotten to where she was by being easily lulled. At twenty-nine, she was the youngest manager in Dominic Laredo's empire—a position she'd held for two years. And her current position would be just the beginning of her professional rise.

But now, less than a week until the most important event of her career, Lily couldn't shake the gnawing dread that some catastrophe was brewing. Why did Dominic Laredo, her boss, have to choose the Isla del Oro for his wedding? Of all his resort sites—and all the other glorious resorts in the world that would love to accommodate him—why had he had to pick hers? She alternated between relishing the chance to shine and wondering what disaster lurked just over the horizon. Previously, she'd been confident she could handle anything that might come up. Now, for the first time in years, she felt the chill breath of doubt and insecurity blowing an unwelcome breeze. She had to get back to her usual mindset pronto.

After all, Lily knew having Dominic Laredo at the Isla del Oro for his big day was a feather in her cap. When he'd announced his plans, the managers of all the other Fantasia resorts sent congratulatory emails—tinged green with jealousy. But her gut kept telling her to watch out. Her career path had been far too smooth—even though she'd worked her tush off for every advance and promotion. Now she had the greatest opportunity to move up to the big time in Dominic Laredo's organization—or to make a monumental ass of herself. Though she nearly rivaled her boss in her attention to the most minute of details, she kept thinking there was something she was just plain overlooking.

If she weren't keeping herself on a twenty-four/seven alert, she'd pour some chilled white wine to calm her nerves. Oh hell, she knew what she really needed—the right man to take her in his arms and love away her doubts. At this point, maybe she didn't even need him to be the *right* man in any of the usual meanings of that word—as long as he was right to cure what ailed her now.

Lily grinned to herself as her Cherokee grandmother came to mind. Old Alma had been cool, especially when she'd taught Lily about the care, feeding, and uses of men. Lily wished she could phone Alma right now, just to hear her calming words. But Alma was on her honeymoon in Hawaii with her fourth husband—and inaccessible for all but the most urgent of reasons. Horniness and nerves didn't qualify. Thoughts of her grandmother's recent marriage to a man twenty years her junior gave Lily a chuckle. Alma, having outlived her first three husbands, had chosen this time to wed one with some staying power.

Her grandmother had a more impressive track record than Lily when it came to men. In her career-building, Lily had relegated relationships to second level priority, just like the other major influence on her life, Aunt Dolores. By age thirty, Dolores was CEO of a large food manufacturing conglomerate. Now in her fifties, Dolores was wealthy, successful—but profoundly alone. Lily absolutely believed that she could learn from both Alma and Dolores and have it all—the career and the love.

But right now Lily seemed to be following in Dolores's lonely footsteps. Lily's memories of her last…involvement, for want of a better word…made her frown. Though she hadn't expected commitment from Bert Stone, she'd demanded exclusivity. When she'd come back to her office after a business meeting to find him screwing her assistant on Lily's desk... Not only was that the end of Bert, but she'd also had to get a new assistant and a new desk. And Lily had been fond of both.

Damn, she missed him right now. Bert had known how to take her mind off business when she needed a break. There'd been no one since Bert, more than six months earlier. She wanted a superb lover who treated her with, in the words of the immortal Aretha, R-E-S-P-E-C-T. And TLC. Because at this moment, Lily's responsibilities and her horniness were rubbing her nerve endings raw.

But she had to get her mind off those nerve endings and that horniness so she could focus fully on Dominic Laredo's wedding. She'd reviewed all the plans seventeen hundred and fifty-six times. To give herself a shot at getting some sleep tonight, she'd review those plans for the seventeen hundred and fifty-seventh time. And maybe later she'd try out the brand new vibrator that had arrived in the day's mail.

So she read the wedding timetable and details over, checking off everything that was complete, noting what still needed attention. She looked up for a moment as starlight glinting in through the window reflected off Winnie, her bedroom desk owl. Lily liked to keep her huge collection of owls around her at home and at work. Her wisdom and love of order must have come from her owl nature. Which was often at war with her tiger nature, the only bequest she had from her long-gone father, Alfredo Tiger. She blamed him for the impatient masculine energy that had her twitching to call it a night. Owl won, and she settled in to work some more.

By two a.m. Wednesday, Lily had done everything she could. She yawned, stretched, and let her gaze wander over to her new vibrator. She picked it up, closed her eyes, and turned it on. It turned her on with its rhythmic vibrations in the palm of her hand. She turned it off and brought it with her when she crawled into bed. Tonight she enjoyed the feel of her smooth, cool, white-on-white silk sheets against her tired, overheated muscles.

Still tightly wound, Lily got the vibrator off her night table, pressed the button, and listened as it buzzed its song. Lily fingered her already moist, too long neglected pussy, then began to massage with her brand new toy. Her soft pink folds grew slicker, more than ready to accommodate her plastic friend. Despite her fatigue, Lily gave herself up to the mounting sensations emanating from her hungry core. As she massaged herself, she felt some of her long-held tension begin to dissipate. While she relaxed from her work problems, a different, more delicious tension took over. She tightened her legs and began to move faster as the longed-for orgasm began to grow. Lily loved the freedom she got from the isolation of her cottage. She could bounce on her bedsprings and sigh and gasp and make all the noise she ever wanted without concern for anyone hearing. Too bad there was no guy here making noises with her. Still, tonight she took advantage of her solitude to pant out her frustration and need, her release, as the vibrator took her up and over the crest of a short but very delicious come. Lily sighed, put aside the plastic toy, and closed her eyes.

And suddenly opened them as the details of the upcoming wedding reasserted themselves. The Parisian head chef and the Hollywood florist were scheduled to arrive first thing Thursday morning on Dominic's private jet. Several hours afterward, a chartered cargo jet would arrive from New York with the special foods and flowers Dominic had personally ordered. The chef and the florist would oversee the unloading and all the handling of the imported foods and flowers. If all went as it should, Lily wouldn't have much face-to-face time working with the chef and florist before the goods arrived. But she'd worked hard to set up communication lines among all the people who'd be working together to make the wedding happen. She'd had quite a job convincing the resident chefs and florists to share their turf with Dominic's imported honchos. But so far she'd managed to massage everyone's ego.

A small army of workers would also be arriving on Thursday, along with many of the three hundred wedding guests, and, oh yeah, Dominic Laredo and Gwyn Verde. Lily had managed to arrange reasonable accommodations for everyone, no small feat, but she still needed to check on a few last minute details that had arisen.

By the time she finished reviewing all the arrangements yet again, Lily's stress was back full force. There was no way she could function the next day without sleep. She reached to her bedside table again for her new purple companion, which she'd named Vincenzo. Vincenzo would put her to sleep. Vincenzo knew all the places that needed touching, rubbing. Within moments, Vincenzo was slick from Lily's orgasm. She put Vincenzo away and sighed. She needed to find a man soon. Or else buy more batteries...

Lily picked up Sophia, the little Italian marble owl she kept on her night table. Though she loved every owl in her collection, Sophia and Blanca, the plush white snow owl she kept between her pillows, were her favorites. When she got through Dominic's wedding, she'd treat herself to another owl — maybe two. And a vacation. A short one. Well, maybe not a vacation, not even a short one. But at least one new owl. She picked up the white snow owl and cuddled it to her as she fell asleep.

* * * * *

Once the plane bound for Miami was airborne, Pete booted up his laptop, plugged in to the air phone system, and dialed up his home office. Someone might catch his scheme in time to undo it. After several clicks on the keyboard, he saw that all systems were go. At the appointed hour, all Laredo's special orders would be consigned to an obscure Never Never Land. He disconnected and put his laptop to sleep, then wished he could do the same for himself. He sat back as far as possible in his tiny coach seat and stretched his long legs out, having to pull them back from the aisle every time someone went by. Forget sleep. He hated being scrunched up in the tiny "economy" seats. Gwyn wasn't flying coach any more these days. With Laredo, she'd be going first class all the way—or by private jet. Well, she might be flying first class, but their wedding would be not even third-rate.

Revenge was turning out to be easy. Laredo insisted on importing masses of food and flowers for the wedding. Of course. Pete volunteered to his supervisor, who wasn't aware of Pete's connection to Gwyn, to arrange for the delivery. Then Pete made just one *tiny* error in the itinerary for Laredo's jet. Pete simply keyed in an 's' instead of an 'r', a typo which could happen to anyone. Thus he'd routed several hundred thousand dollars' worth of gourmet foods and fancy flowers to the Isla del *Oso*, not the Isla del *Oro*. Instead of going to the Caribbean, all

Laredo's expensive, perishable cargo would end up on a remote island off the coast of Chile.

Pete patted himself on the back. The sheer simplicity of his scheme only enhanced its brilliance. By the time anyone would discover the mix-up, it would be far too late to correct. Aside from the distance between the two islands, the goods, including such delicacies as fifty-dollar-a-pound beef from Scotland, were far too spoilable to survive their being dumped in primitive storage facilities. So Dominic Laredo's wedding would be a piss-poor party with an inadequate supply of food and flowers. Laredo would be exposed, very publicly and very definitively, for the loser he was.

It would serve Laredo right to feel like a loser, for once. The way Pete had been feeling for months.

Pete's groin tightened at the thought of Gwyn begging to come back to him. He frowned a bit. Okay, so he hadn't worked this part out perfectly. Gwyn was pretty mad when she dumped him, and often before that. So maybe Pete would have to prove to her that he'd changed. That he'd learned what she wanted him to, though he wasn't exactly sure what that was. But Pete would work that out. He'd have to if he intended her to stay with him once she came back. He shifted in his seat. Once he had her with him again, he knew he could somehow be more responsive to her needs so that she'd never again want to leave.

The plane touched down just as the last rays of daylight faded. After getting his bearings in the noisy airport, Pete caught a shuttle to his motel. He took about three minutes to settle into his nondescript motel room, then dialed out for another check on the laptop. Everything was going fine.

Pete was not used to having a free evening. Tonight he couldn't even just hang with the Lost Boys — or Griselda. The long hours of the night stretched before him. He channel-surfed and found he had his choice between news, weather info, stale sitcoms, and old movies. What did people do for fun around here? If he stayed in his room, he'd probably be climbing the walls by ten o'clock Miami time — seven on his internal clock.

According to the TV listings, championship mud wrestling wouldn't come on for another two hours. Nothing else snagged him. So Pete took himself down to the bar off the motel lobby. He'd treat himself to a brew and get some dinner.

At the bar's entrance, pink plastic flamingos — possibly Griselda's avian cousins — cavorted under swaying palms on a paper mural. Three guys, tired business travelers trying to sell the wrong products, sat on stools, drank beer, munched peanuts, and exchanged occasional small talk. The bartender, a redhead who looked like she'd been around the block one too many times, frowned as she mixed a drink while two TV pundits blared out their dissection of the afternoon's ball game. Pete sat at the end of the bar farthest away from the businessmen and ordered a Dos Equis.

"Where 'ya from?" the bartender, whose nametag identified her as Nan, asked.

"San Diego," Pete grunted.

"Pretty city," she said. When she smiled, Nan looked a bit less haggard. "So why's a California guy coming to Miami? Can't be pleasure, so it must be business, right?"

"Right," Pete said, raising his glass in mock salute.

Nan glanced down the bar at the other customers. No one else appeared to need her immediate services. "Are you buying or selling here in Miami?"

Pete toyed with the idea of making up some response, then decided it wasn't worth the effort. "Neither. I'll be catching a plane to Puerto Rico in the morning." He downed a big swallow of his beer.

"Puerto Rico? What are you going to…"

He cut her off. "Hey, Nan. No business talk tonight, at least not about me. So, you been in Miami long?"

"Just since my old man split, three years now. We lived in Minnesota." She shook her head.

"Minnesota?" Pete chuckled. "That's quite a change."

Nan shrugged. "I had more than enough cold gray winters to last me two lifetimes. And I can see all the snow I want in photos. I look at them, and when I get tired, I shut the book." Nan wiped the already spotless counter with a cloth.

Pete took another sip of his beer and studied her. "So why Miami instead of, say, San Diego?"

She rubbed her fingers together indicating cash. "It's way cheaper to live here, otherwise I'd be out there in a shot. I always dreamed of living in California." Her eyes took on a faraway look, and she seemed almost pretty in an older woman way.

He nodded. One of the businessmen signaled Nan for a refill. Two more men and a woman entered the bar. The various conversations began to liven up the place. Pete watched Nan as she gracefully and efficiently went about her job. He was surprised to realize he found her company a reasonable distraction from his restlessness.

When she'd served everyone, Nan looked over at Pete who nodded that yes, he'd like a refill. He smiled, signaling he'd also enjoy her company. Actually, at this point he preferred her company to the beer. Pete dipped into the basket of nuts and pretzels Nan had left earlier. His stomach rumbled, and Pete became aware that he was hungry for more than bar munchies. He'd just swallowed his second handful when Nan brought his beer, which he left untouched.

"So what time do you get off tonight?" Pete asked, surprising himself with his question.

Nan appeared equally surprised — and pleased. She looked at her watch. "The other bartender comes on in half an hour. It being so quiet here tonight, I could probably leave in an hour or so, after she gets settled." Nan blushed, which Pete found charming.

"Would you come out with me for some dinner? I hate to eat alone."

A flicker of what almost looked like disappointment passed over her face. "I could fix you a sandwich here at the bar or get you a burger and fries from the grill."

Pete's stomach rumbled again, this time so loud Nan had to hear it. "A burger and fries sounds great," he said. Seeing her look expectantly at him, he added, "I'd still like you to leave with me when you can." He'd have liked to eat with her, but he was too hungry to postpone his meal any longer.

Nan lowered her lashes and smiled. "You've got it. Now let me get that order in for you. They'll send it over right away. How do you like your burger?"

"Medium, ketchup, and onions. Lots of fries. You have those curly ones?"

"Just the long kind."

"That'll do."

Nan spoke the order into an intercom, then waited on some other customers. Pete watched her bend over, revealing excellent legs as her short pink uniform skirt rode up to within inches of tight round buns. Pete shifted as he felt his groin tighten. He'd never been with an older woman, not in any way. But something about Nan appealed to him. Her being clearly so much older almost added an air of exoticism, as if her age were some foreign country or unusual ethnicity.

She soon brought him a plate with a huge burger and an impressive order of fries. As he was still nursing his second beer, Pete said he didn't want anything else to drink. He saw Nan watching him while he ate. The burger tasted unusually delicious, as if he hadn't eaten for days. Was it Nan's eyes on him that heightened its flavor? As the meat's juices flowed into him, Pete felt a reawakening of his senses—which had been hibernating since when? Since Gwyn had left him? Had it really been so long since anything had tasted—or looked—so good to him?

The fries stood up to the burger in quality. Crispy on the outside, soft inside, salted and herbed to perfection. He held out his plate to Nan, offering her a fry. "Not when I'm on duty," she said, her voice low and sultry.

Pete savored his impromptu meal, relishing every morsel of the food, feeling satisfied when he'd gobbled the final fry and sipped the last of his beer. Nan's counterpart, a young graduate student named Maya, arrived early and was more than willing for Nan to leave before the official end of her shift.

"Thanks, darlin'. I owe you one," Nan said to Maya.

Maya waved dismissively. "Have a great time. See you tomorrow."

"Give me just a minute to change," Nan said to Pete, walking into a room marked Employees Only. True to her word, she stepped out moments later having changed from her pink uniform to black slacks and a white pullover.

Now Pete realized he didn't know where to take Nan. He couldn't just ask her up to his room... "Where can we go to be alone and talk?"

"I know a little club where we could listen to some music," she said, giving her hair a pat and taking his arm to walk out.

"Sounds great. Uh, how do we get there?"

She smiled at him. "In my car," she said, leading him over to an ancient lime green VW Bug with daisies painted on its doors.

Pete climbed in and got comfortable in the little car. Nan drove with assurance, getting them to a strip mall in ten minutes. Pete was relieved to find that, just as advertised, Nan was taking him to a small place, just a few tables and a simple bar. Tonight a pianist played jazz improvisations softly in the background.

"I've had enough of being at a bar for tonight," Nan said. A hostess led them to a table for two in the corner farthest from the piano. A server came over to get their orders. Though he wasn't going to drink much more, Pete got another beer, Nan a margarita.

"Thanks for coming out with me," Pete said.

Nan looked him in the eyes. "How old are you, Pete?"

He scowled. "Why?"

She laughed dryly. "I don't even know your last name or what kind of work you do. Look at me asking your age first." She shrugged. "Just one of my Midwest hang-ups, I guess."

Pete found Nan more and more appealing with each word she said. "Payne. P-A-Y-N-E. A computer geek. Still want to know how old I am?" he asked, reaching out to take her hand in his.

"Yes," she said softly.

"I'm thirty. How much does it matter?"

"Sullivan. A potter and a bartender. Fifty-two. How much does it matter to you?"

Pete grinned easily. "Not at all." He found he actually meant what he said. He traced the lines in her left palm with his index finger. "Nan Sullivan, I'm glad I met you."

The server's arrival with their drinks briefly intruded on the growing warmth between them. Pete found it both soothing and exciting to have Nan with him—and time off from his obsession with Gwyn. "To older women," he said, raising his beer stein in salute.

"And younger men." She clinked her margarita glass against his stein.

They both chuckled and drank, Nan deeply, Pete very little.

"So you're heading off to Puerto Rico in the morning," Nan said. "Will you be coming back this way when your business is done?"

Pete shook his head. "No such plans...at this time. Except to pass through again."

She nodded and took another sip of her drink. "So, how long will it take you to finish what you're doing in Puerto Rico?"

The last thing Pete wanted to talk or think about now was the Isla del Oro project, as he'd labeled it in his head. How could he steer the conversation elsewhere than Nan's perfectly reasonable questions? Gwyn's complaints that he rarely asked about her suddenly popped into his mind. And Pete was vaguely aware that women liked to talk about themselves. Hell, women liked to talk, period. Well, might as well give that a try. So he shook his head again. "Don't want to talk about that. Would much rather hear about you, Nan."

She shrugged. "Familiar story. Was married for twenty-five years to my high school sweetheart. Our wedding was the day after I graduated. He was a year ahead of me. We had four kids together—and now two grandchildren with a third on the way. It all ended three years ago. Jerry, that was my husband, had the typical mid-life crisis. Found his way through it by climbing into the sack with his twenty-three year old secretary." She began shredding a cocktail napkin. "They're now the proud parents of twin boys." She laughed dryly. "Jerry's doing diaper duty. His wife must be quite a woman if she gets him to do that." She tore the last of the napkin, then pushed the debris into a small pile alongside her drink.

Pete was finding he actually liked the process of getting to know this woman, and not just so he could get her in the sack. "Obviously a man of limited intelligence and taste."

Nan smiled. "I like to think so. My oldest daughter moved down here to Miami four years ago. She invited me to her house for some R and R after Jerry... When I'd wept my last tear, I decided to move here to be with her and her family and start living *la vida loca*. Though I'll tell you, if I had the bucks, I'd have gone to San Diego. But here I am." Her voice trailed off.

"You said you're a potter as well as a bartender?"

Nan grinned broadly. "A hobby I want to turn into a business. I used to make dishes, vases, that sort of thing, at the Y. Always gave them to friends and family for Christmas. I figured everyone was just humoring me when they acted happy to get my stuff." She blushed. "Imagine my surprise when people began asking me to make different pieces for them. I never thought a person could turn something they love doing into a business. I'm in the process of learning how to do that."

"I bet you'll be great," he said, and meant it. "So where does that bartending fit in?"

"I call it my day job at night. Helps pay the bills 'til the pottery catches on."

"My money's on you. I bet you hit it big soon."

"From your mouth to God's ear," Nan said, toasting him again.

"Come back to my room with me, Nan Sullivan. Stay with me tonight."

Grinning, she stood up and flung her purse over her shoulder. "I thought you'd never ask."

Chapter Two

Pete put his arm around Nan, and they walked quickly to her car. Nan felt...soft. Her body felt as tender to him as he'd expected, looking at her lush curves. She wasn't at all his usual type—Gwyn, a slim, gorgeous blonde, had been that. Maybe it was time to change his type. Just for tonight, he vowed to banish Gwyn from his thoughts. Tonight Nan—with her brassy red hair, her brown puppy dog eyes, her bright red lipsticked mouth, and her generous body—was all the woman he'd need or want. He gazed at her profile in the night-darkened car as she drove them to the motel.

By the time they'd driven back to the motel, gotten out of the car and up to his room, and he'd opened his door, Pete's erection was good to go. Of course he'd never had any problems getting it up, and he was pleased to see that his sexual hiatus from real women hadn't adversely affected his equipment. Any problems he'd had were in other areas. He remembered only too well Gwyn's frequent—and vocal—dissatisfaction with him. *Maybe you should have listened more*, a voice he'd have preferred not to hear whispered in him. He willed it to go away.

Of course, after all this time without a real woman, the first time would probably be a classic slam-bam-thank-you-ma'am. Gwyn always hated those, called him selfish. Well, only when he came fast and then had to leave her. She hadn't at all seemed to mind when he'd spent more time with her, taken things slower, and he'd been more attentive. But Gwyn had always taken it personally when he, as he put it, came and ran.

Looking at Nan now, Pete sensed that beneath her experienced and world-weary demeanor lay a deep vulnerability. Like she could be really hurt if he messed up with her. And he didn't want to hurt her. Not when she was being so nice, keeping him from having to spend this long night alone. And hell, she trusted him enough to go with him even after her asshole of a husband had screwed up her life so thoroughly. No, he had to treat this woman right. Maybe there was some cosmic score sheet where he'd get points with Gwyn if he helped this woman feel good tonight.

Pete's hand shook a bit as he slipped the key card into the door. He wished he had a nicer room to bring her to. "I'm sorry, this isn't much," he said, waving his hands around and hoping she didn't get freaked at the sight of his raging erection.

Nan put down her purse and shook her head. "I work at this joint." She looked around. "Trust me on this, Pete. You have the super deluxe suite here."

She was a really kind lady. Imagine her trying to make him feel better about bringing her to such a dump. Pete took Nan in his arms and pulled her close. She smelled like citrus, tangy with a hint of something sweet. Nan hugged him, gently molding her body against his. He started to kiss her gently, and then his cock took command of his thinking processes and he thrust his tongue deeper into her sweet mouth. More of that subtle citrus flavor. After a momentary hesitation, Nan's showed her hunger for his kisses with some inventive tongue action of her own.

Pete had known it wouldn't take much to get him going. His erection was jammed tight against Nan's soft belly, and he needed to be in her—soon. He wanted to be naked with her now. But he knew he couldn't just pull off her clothing. He'd undress first. "Let's get naked," he murmured.

While an amazed Nan stood there watching him, Pete jumped out of his clothes.

She gasped, her eyes wide at the sight of him. Pete knew she'd seen naked men before, and he'd been told he was easy on the eyes. He looked at her questioningly. Maybe she really wasn't ready yet.

"You certainly get down to business fast," Nan said, now averting her eyes.

Pete winced. *Fast* was one of those words Gwyn had used when she meant *no good*. His mind scrambled to think of what to do next. "Should I put on some clothes?" he asked hoarsely, feeling genuinely confused. He knew they'd both end up naked together, didn't particularly see any value in moving backward.

To his surprise, Nan said, "Yes, please."

He stood frozen, his erection subsiding a fraction.

"It's not that you're not gorgeous," she said quickly. "And many women would be thrilled to have a chance to look at you. But it's hard for me to think when you're standing there…like that." She blushed.

He wiggled his eyebrows and said, "Thinking's not required." Nonetheless, he threw on his T-shirt and his Spiderman boxers. Then he went over to her, took her in his arms, and nuzzled her gently.

She felt so good to him, warm and giving in his arms. His erection was back to full force. "Thank you for coming with me tonight," he murmured, meaning each word.

"You thanked me already," she said, pulling slightly away.

He drew her closer. "I can't thank you enough. I really didn't want to be alone."

"Nor I," she whispered, putting her arms around his waist and burrowing her head into his chest.

Pete put his hand under her chin and raised her face so he could kiss her. Despite the demands of his hard, hungry cock, he began his kiss with great tenderness. Her lips were full and smooth, sweet to his taste, parting easily to his questing tongue. She met his kiss with a gentleness matching his own, and then her fervor grew in sync with his. They both clutched each other more tightly as their kiss deepened in intensity. They broke apart, and she moaned. Or was it he?

They stayed apart for mere seconds while Pete devoured her lovely face with his eyes. And then they found their way back into each other's arms—and kissed with a sense of growing amazement at finding themselves together in this place at this time.

Pete slid his hand under Nan's shirt and cupped her breast, impatient at the barrier of her bra. Nan flinched away from him. "What is it?" he asked, stunned by her sudden movement.

Nan folded her arms in front of her then turned away.

Pete had never before felt so confused. He tried to face her, but she kept turning away from him. What had he done wrong this time? "Please," he pleaded with her, "please tell me what's happened."

Nan's eyes filled with tears. Damn, he'd fucked up already—and didn't even know how or what. Maybe he'd squeezed her too hard. Or maybe he'd misunderstood... Though he was sure he couldn't be that off in reading her signals. "Aw, Nan. I'm sorry," he said, gently wiping the tears from her face. "What'd I do? And what can I do to make it better?"

She snuffled, wiped her eyes, and shook her head. "It's not you."

"Then what?" he asked, stymied.

She took a deep breath. "My body," she stammered at last.

"Your body?" he repeated, forcing himself to keep looking her in the eyes. "What about your body, Nan?"

Another sniffle. "I don't want you to look at my body."

Pete couldn't believe what she was saying. He hadn't done anything wrong, at least not yet. She had her own issues. "You're beautiful," he said automatically, wanting to get his hands on her boobs and his cock into her.

Her lips pursed and her eyes brimming with disappointment, she gave him a "come on, don't bullshit me" look. But then he realized she really was beautiful to him right at that moment. Well, maybe not exactly *beautiful* in the classic sense, but something really wonderful.

And it was more than the sex, though that was driving him crazy too. Pete's mind flashed back to when he was a scrawny sixteen-year-old whose sex life consisted of wet dreams. Too shy to even talk to girls. To celebrate getting his driver's license, his buddies bought him a visit to the neighborhood ho' house. Scared, knees shaking, but out-of-his-mind horny, Pete entered the small room where

Roseann plied her trade. Roseann with the big boobs, the blonde hair above and dark below, who'd smelled like the flower she was named for. All he wanted in the world was to get his cock into her and have her squeal with delight. She squealed, all right. With suppressed laughter. One look at him and she rolled her eyes, snapped her gum, and warned him they had to get the whole business over in fifteen minutes so she could go on to her next john.

Once he got inside her, it was more like fifteen seconds.

Of course he'd bragged to his buddies how great it was. If only she'd said one kind word to him...something.

Remembering Roseann, Pete wished he had a whole different set of words to convince Nan of how he felt. One thing he knew—none of the words at his disposal and none of his previous experiences had prepared him for being here at this time with this woman. And that made him even sadder than the thought that they might not end up having sex after all.

She laughed harshly and pulled herself away from him. "Pete, you're a nice guy, but this was a really bad idea. My coming here. I thought I could just go off with you, act like some pick-up tart. What the hell? You're from way out of town—a classic one-night stand. But I can't do this. I want to go home. Now." She started straightening her clothes, her hair.

"Nan, don't go, not like that," he said softly. "Hell, I want you to stay." Pete tried to think what he could possibly do to change her mind—and banish that hurt look from her eyes. Then he got a brilliant idea. He'd be honest—and treat her the way he'd always wished Roseann had. "Nan, I've been with lots of women."

"I figured that out," she snapped. "No need to brag."

Great. His attempt at honesty bombed. He needed to explain what he meant before things went even more downhill. "I'm not bragging. I've been with lots of women, but they've all dumped me. Some sooner, some later." He cupped her chin in his hand.

"Hard to believe," she said, her voice sounding muffled.

"It's true. And Gwyn, the last one, hurt the most. I think I'm supposed to be getting a message here, but I must be too dense. So, Nan, tell me what to do."

"You think I know better than you?"

He nodded. "Oh, yeah. What do women want, Nan? What do *you* want?" He'd listen, really listen, to what she had to say.

She moved away from him and sat down on the bed. "You really want me to tell you, don't you?"

"More than anything else in the world." For the moment, that was exactly true.

She laughed dryly. "What I want is impossible. You see, Pete, I wish you could transport me back in time. See me the way I was. I don't want to sag here and here," she said, viciously poking her breasts and her stomach. "I want to be young and lovely for you."

Pete wished he could somehow snap his fingers and produce what she wanted—for her sake, not his. He sat down next to her, took her hand in his, and kissed her palm. "I can't turn time back, and I wouldn't want to. You are lovely to me. Exactly as you are now. I wouldn't change anything about you. How can I prove that to you?"

She shook her head. "You really are crazy, you know?"

"You're not the first person to say so. But you didn't answer my question. Even a crazy guy deserves to have his questions answered."

She sighed. "I wish you could put a mask on, blinders, so you wouldn't see what a wreck I've become." She bit her lip.

He ran his fingertips over her face. "I don't want to miss a moment of being with you as you are now. You're lovely to me. Let me show you how much." He kissed her tenderly. She sighed.

"I want you to get naked with me, Nan," he whispered, gently pushing back a tendril of hair curling around her ear. "I want to touch you and see you and taste you and smell you and hear you. I want to be with you in every way a man can be with a woman."

She kissed her fingertips and touched them to his face. "Oh, Pete," she said. "I haven't been with any man since...since Jerry left."

He nodded. "Nan, I'm honored to be the first. And we have this in common. I also haven't been with a woman since...well, since Gwyn, my almost-fiancée, dumped me. Left me for my billionaire boss. So, in a sense, you'll be my first, too."

Nan took a deep shuddery breath and rose. For a moment, Pete was afraid she'd decided to leave after all. But she kicked off her sandals. And then she pulled off her shirt and pants—and stood before him in white lacy bra and yellow flowered panties. His erection grew more solid. "You're beautiful," he breathed, wanting to crush her in his arms and kiss her everywhere.

She didn't look as if she believed him completely, but she turned around, unhooked her bra, and, in stripper fashion, tossed it to him. He caught the bra and forced himself to remain seated on the bed while she slowly turned around to face him.

His eyes grew wide as he took in her breasts—large, with big dark nipples that faced down rather than out. He wanted to get his hands on those breasts and his mouth on her nipples. His cock began to throb. "May I touch you?" he breathed.

Nan slowly nodded her assent. "Yes," she said. "Oh, yes."

Pete went over to where she was standing. Nan was so much shorter, he had to splay his long legs and bend to be able to engulf her nipple in his eager mouth. As he explored her breasts with nimble fingers, his cock grew more insistent. He longed to plunge himself into her warmth, but he knew he had to pace himself with her.

Nan reached her hands around Pete, digging her fingernails into his back and pulling him more tightly to her. Her nipples hardened into stiff peaks as Pete licked and gently nibbled. They both moaned. Pete was afraid he'd come in midair, before he even got anywhere near being inside her. Not that it would be a problem for him to get hard again—but coming like that was so junior high.

With great difficulty he drew away from her. She looked up at him. He slipped his fingers into the elastic at the top of her panties, with his eyes asked her permission to proceed. She made a slight nod with her head to let him know it was okay. He resisted the impulse to tear the panties from her. Instead, he slid them down slowly, past her glorious triangle, thick with curling brown hair, past her soft thighs, past her knees, and then he helped her step out of them. For a moment, she shivered in a nonexistent breeze, looking at him, her eyes filled with longing and a questioning concern.

He answered by lowering himself to his knees, then burying his face in the curly brown hair at the junction of her legs and inhaling her sultry scent. After an initial move to pull back, Nan pressed her slick pink folds to Pete, spreading her legs and holding his head to her. "Oh, Pete," she sighed, creating shivers up and down his spine.

He had to get her into the bed. Now. Reluctantly pulling back from her hot, wet core, he rose and scooped her up in his arms. Vulnerable as a rag doll, she draped her arms around his neck and nuzzled her head under his chin.

Even in his erotic haze, Pete realized Nan was not a woman to just throw down on the bed, so he laid her down as gently as he could and kissed her. Then all restraint evaporated as he hopped onto the bed next to her and pulled her into a tight embrace. Cripes, she practically sucked his cock into her glistening pussy the moment he stretched out facing her.

So much for foreplay. He climbed on top of her, then held back for a moment, asking, "Is this okay?" She moaned her assent and opened her legs further. He wanted to plunge into her with total abandon. A condom. Shit, he must have brought a condom with him. Don't leave home without it. Oh, that was a credit card. Pete's brain raced, or rather jolted. He pulled back from Nan. She sat up, her eyes wide as saucers.

Pete stroked her back, wanting to reassure her that nothing was wrong. Other than his lack of a condom. "Uh, I have to check in my wallet for…" he said.

She smiled smugly. "In my bag," she said, making a vague hand wave in the direction of the table where she'd thrown her purse. "I always carry some with me. My friends call me an optimistic dreamer," she added hoarsely.

Pete's respect for Nan ratcheted up several notches, and so did his desire. He leapt off the bed, flew to her purse, and brought it back to her. Nan winked at him, then pulled out a fistful of the vital foil packages. Despite the trembling of his fingers, he managed to tear the foil open, wrap his throbbing cock, and pull her back to him with eager arms.

"Thanks for being prepared," Pete murmured, kissing Nan. He touched her pussy, amazed and gratified that she was so hot and wet and ready for him. Now he inserted one finger, then a second into her moist sheath. Nan moaned. Pete couldn't wait a moment longer.

After stroking her brown curls and the sensitive skin of her vee, Pete positioned the head of his cock at the entrance to Nan's waiting slit and thrust. She wiggled her substantial hips and wrapped her legs around him, clamping her hands on his butt as if she never wanted to let go. And they began to move together, falling into a mutually satisfying rhythm. Their sighs of relief and pleasure mingled with the creak of the bed and the friction of skin against skin.

Pete knew he'd be coming real fast, real hard, and real abundantly. Despite his hand jobs and, of course, Griselda, he was sure he'd managed to store up gallons of cum—just waiting for the release of being with a woman. He visualized himself exploding like a volcano, a geyser hot from the earth's core. Oh, yeah. Nan moved against him just right.

Gwyn had always complained that he thought only of himself, especially when he was about to come. His jaw tightened and he felt a slowing of his relentless march to orgasm. Right now he was all about proving to Gwyn how wrong she'd been.

Maybe he should start by focusing on Nan. "How is it for you, baby?" he asked. Had he just called a fifty-two year old woman *baby*?

"Oh, God," Nan said, digging her nails into his back.

Evidently he hadn't offended her. "Anything you want me to do different?" he growled, his excitement growing as he felt her urging him on to go deeper and harder.

"Maybe a little slower," she said, sounding breathless.

Slower. That wasn't how he'd have interpreted the signals of her hands on his back, but the lady had said the word. He swallowed hard and consciously tried to slow down, savoring the feel of Nan's muscles rippling along the length of his cock, trying not to savor it too much. This focus so close to a climax was a whole new experience for him. Not particularly easy, but he could see the effort might pay off.

Slow, slow, and then there it was. Too long denied, his orgasm was about to rip off the top of his head. No way he could stop it. Not a moment longer could he hold himself back. Pete cried out with the power of his release and, as he'd expected, felt himself pump out an amazing amount of fluid.

Good as he felt, a moment later he also felt bad—sure she must have been disappointed. Nan was stroking his back, murmuring words of nonsense.

He kissed her neck and hugged her. "Was that all right for you?" A lot depended on her answer.

She sighed.

He raised himself up and looked at her, then withdrew carefully. "Did you come?" he asked, though he knew she hadn't.

"Oh, Pete," she said softly, "it was wonderful."

She sounded happy and she looked content, but he wasn't going to let her get away without answering. "Did you come?" he asked again, determined to get an answer. A woman would never have to ask him the same question. His orgasms were out there for the entire world to see, hear, feel, and heck, even to taste.

"Why?" she asked, a slight frown creasing her forehead.

"It's important for me to know." He looked her straight in the eyes.

She sighed again. "Not exactly," she admitted at last.

Just what he'd suspected. A ripple of discomfort flashed through him. "You either did or you didn't," Pete said, rolling off to lie next to her.

Now she looked miserable, and that wasn't what he wanted. "It's been such a long time for me... I don't know if I remember how..."

Pete scowled. "I thought it was like riding a bike—you know, you don't forget."

She fluttered her hands and chuckled. "I never did learn how to ride a bike."

Pete wasn't going to let himself be mollified or let go easily. "My last girlfriend always complained. Said I didn't satisfy her, wasn't romantic. And then she dumped me."

For Pete's Sake

Nan sat up and pulled the sheet up to cover her breasts. "Really? She didn't find you romantic?"

"Yeah." He sat up next to her.

Nan thought for several moments. "Pete, do you want to know what I think—based on our very short time together and my very limited experience with men other than my husband?"

What the hell. He might as well hear the worst. He was a bedroom failure. The kind of guy people told nasty jokes about. Roseann was predicting his future when she laughed. "Yeah. Nan, I want you to be totally honest."

"I suppose I can do that—being we'll never see each other again after tonight." She leaned back more fully against the pillows and turned to him.

Pete thought this would be the time to light up—if either of them had been smokers. "Who knows? Maybe we'll see each other again…"

"Hush," she said, reaching up and putting her finger to this mouth. "No bullshit between us. Okay?"

"Agreed."

"First of all, romance and satisfying your woman in bed are two things that go together but aren't exactly the same. I'd guess what your girlfriend wanted was for you to be more thoughtful—to think more about what she might want than maybe you did."

"Ex-girlfriend," Pete said gruffly. "Otherwise, based on what she always said, you probably have it just about right." He'd been half hoping Nan would tell him how perfect he was—and how unreasonable Gwyn must have been. It didn't sound like that was the direction Nan was going. Well, she'd said she wasn't going to bullshit him.

"Pete Payne," she continued, "I want to thank you for tonight. You see, being with you is like a first step for me. Now I can go on with my life, knowing a gorgeous, what's the word—hunky?—young man found me attractive."

What was this crap? Pete couldn't believe the way Nan was almost putting herself down. As if he'd be the only guy who'd find her attractive. "You're more than attractive," he said. "Don't sell yourself short."

She laughed harshly. "I won't. Not any more. But I'll tell you, Pete. Being with you sets the standard real high for the next man who comes along. And now I feel confident there'll be one." She took his hand and put it on her heart. "Pete, I want you to know how special you are. Oh, I imagine you have a few rough edges yet, and maybe not enough practice in reading what your lady needs. But you've got great potential, and you care. You're going to be very special in some lucky woman's life."

Nan's words fell on Pete's ears like soothing drops of cream. A thought niggled at his addled brain, but he couldn't quite get his mind around it. Doubts about how everything had gone down with Gwyn. According to Nan, Pete had something to offer a woman. Maybe lots to offer. Gwyn's loss for not sticking around. And, oh yeah, her wedding would be really messed up. But if he'd really been less than what she wanted or needed... Well, she'd been justified in leaving him. He'd have to fix whatever that was to keep her with him, once she came back, and being with Nan had given him some clue how to do that.

If Gwyn came back.

Damn, his head was spinning. But he could sort all that out tomorrow, when he got to the Isla del Oro. For tonight, he had a sweet, soft woman in his bed, a woman who thought he was hot and special. A woman who thought she'd forgotten how to come. It suddenly became very important to bring her full satisfaction—to have her come so hard they'd both be swinging from the ceiling light fixture.

Pete turned to Nan and said, "You want to use some more of those condoms?"

Nan laughed, reached over to her purse still lying on the night table, and brought over several more. Pete raised an eyebrow, amused and pleased at her continued optimism. He lay down on his back, and, with a whoop, she straddled him. To his utter amazement, she began a downward path of kissing him—starting at his mouth, ending up with his semi-erect penis in her mouth.

His cock quickly grew to a complete erection as she licked, sucked, and kissed him with powerful thrusts of her tongue. He felt her breath hot on him as she cupped his aching balls in her hands, applying pressure that soon had him whimpering with need.

Far too quickly, he felt the stirring of a climax begin. Damn. He couldn't let himself come again without bringing her along for the trip. Though he hated to break the connection, he put his hands on the sides of her face and gently lifted her mouth from him. She looked up, startled. Her lips glistened with the moistness of her eager fellatio.

"Please," he begged, "please, I want to be in you."

She shifted off him and murmured her agreement, removed a condom from its packet, and wrapped him neatly.

"Are you ready?" he asked.

"Oh, yeah," she said, taking his hand and sliding it over her moist slit. She raised her hips and maneuvered herself so she could glide down his throbbing rod, filling her hot sheath with him.

Pete clutched at her delicious rear as Nan began a wild ride. From the noises she was making with her mouth and the sounds of her pussy sliding up and down him, beautiful glopping melodies full of joy, Pete knew he was bringing her pleasure. And the knowledge made him harder, bigger, and more eager than ever to please her. How strange and wonderful that her pleasure increased his. All his senses sprang to new heightened life. The creaking of the bedsprings was like the sexiest of love ballads. Nan's scent vibrated his every olfactory sensor.

She had her legs on his hips, squeezing him, urging him deeper and deeper into her hidden mysteries. And then he heard her breath catch and the muscles of her pussy began to clench rhythmically around him. He thought he'd fly through the ceiling on a wave of ecstasy. Nan gasped and moaned and pushed harder and harder — and then she shrieked a long, piercing cry.

Excited beyond endurance by her obvious climax, Pete quickly reached his own. Amazed that he still had anything left, Pete nonetheless came and came and came some more.

Nan collapsed on top of him, her legs and arms once again straddling him. Pete lay in silence, stunned by how much deeper and richer their lovemaking had been than what he'd ever experienced before. Was *this* what Gwyn had meant? If so, he was beginning to realize that maybe she'd been right to complain. Too bad he'd never really listened.

"I hope you don't have to ask this time," Nan whispered drowsily.

"I know," he said, nuzzling her.

They fell asleep in each other's arms. Pete awoke early the next morning, with a huge erection. He nudged Nan awake, and she was agreeable to what would have to be a quickie. After all, they both had places to go and things to do that morning.

But, as Pete was learning, some things just couldn't be rushed. Their morning lovemaking was tender, sweet, and amazingly satisfying. Nan cut him off before he could say anything sentimental or express any regrets about the way he was passing through her life.

After a last lingering kiss, in danger of missing his connections, Pete rose from the bed refreshed, relaxed, and more than ready to take on the world. He said good-bye to Nan, who chose to stay in bed just a bit longer. One thing he knew, she'd remain in his mind far longer than she spent in his life.

Hard on the heels of this thought was a dawning suspicion that maybe, just maybe, his plot for revenge against Gwyn wasn't the best idea he'd ever had. Maybe the situation had not been as black and white as he previously thought.

And then he looked at the clock and realized he had to rush to make his plane to Puerto Rico. As he hurriedly showered, dressed, and got his things together for the rest of his trip, Pete consciously shook off any second thoughts he was beginning to have about his mission. His plan was in motion, he was on his way to Isla del Oro—and his moment of triumph. This was not time to start second-guessing himself.

And this time, once he was with Gwyn again, he finally had a clue as to what to do to make and keep her happy. She'd never want to dump him again.

* * * * *

Wednesday disappeared in the blink of an eye as Lily Tiger devoted herself to the myriad details of the upcoming wedding. Thursday dawn on the Isla del Oro found Lily already at her desk after a very sleepless night. She was just drinking her second cup of full octane coffee when her phone rang. "Did you clear up the argument between the Hollywood florist and the one from New York?" a familiar voice asked.

Lily knew Dominic was in a time zone where it was still night, but she wasn't surprised to hear her boss's voice. "Got them on the same page yesterday," she assured him.

"Good," he said. "I knew I could count on you. I'd just like to go over several more details…"

His voice broke off, and Lily heard a female voice in the background. She bit back a smile. Rumor had it that Dominic Laredo had more than met his match in Gwyn Verde. Lily was glad.

The next voice that came on was Gwyn's. "I don't know what time it is where you are," she said, yawning, "but we're going back to bed."

Lily chuckled. "It's going on six-thirty here on the Isla del Oro, Ms. Verde."

"That's Gwyn, Lily. And you should go back to bed, too. I'm sure there's nothing left for you two to worry about for the most over-planned wedding in the history of the western world."

"I'm looking forward to seeing you later today, Gwyn."

"We're actually not getting there 'til tomorrow," Gwyn said. "I figure one day before the wedding is plenty of time. After all, thanks to your hard work, all we have to do is show up. I'll remind Dominic of that, after we both get several more hours of sleep. Oh and Lily, I'm going to ask you a huge favor. Do not contact Dominic today, no matter what. Giving the two of us a day off from talking about the wedding is the best possible gift you can give us. Promise me?"

"I'd love to, Gwyn. But, what if something comes up and Dominic is, uh, displeased that I didn't contact him?"

"I take full responsibility. So we'll see you tomorrow. Don't call us today."

"Of course."

Lily had to admit to herself she was relieved they weren't going to arrive until tomorrow, and that she wasn't going to be on the phone with Dominic fifty times that day. She wished she could feel Gwyn Verde's confidence, but she still hadn't shaken her nagging nervousness, so there'd be no more sleep for her now. Funny, when Lily had first heard that Dominic was engaged, after recovering from her shock that one of the five most eligible bachelors in the world was getting ready for the march down the aisle, she'd been afraid he'd turn some poor woman into a doormat. But it sounded like

Gwyn Verde was more than asserting herself, getting Dominic to lighten up a bit.

Well, some. With this morning's call, it looked like Dominic was reverting to his usual attention to detail. Lily understood where he was coming from. She'd be doing the same if she were in his shoes.

Lily finished drinking her coffee and went down for a walk on the beach. This early, it was still quiet. She'd be able to take a long walk and just think, something that felt like a luxury in her hectic life. As she strode across the sand, she mentally reviewed her to-do list for the day. Dominic's chief chef and florist would arrive fairly early. The flowers and foods he'd painstakingly ordered would arrive later. In between, she'd check all the assistants and workers coming on the early afternoon ferry from Puerto Rico. Several vans would transport them to their quarters. And the many guests arriving today would also be efficiently taken to their rooms by various island shuttles. Lily breathed a sigh of relief that everyone had reasonable accommodations. With all the wedding guests and the extra workers, there wasn't a single empty bed left on the island.

Lily picked up a seashell that caught her eye and wondered how her grandmother was doing. Alma adored seashells and always brought back at least one gorgeous one from each trip. Alma and Enrico, her new husband, were due back to their home in Oklahoma from their honeymoon in Hawaii in four days. Lily would be glad when she finally would be able to talk to Alma. Maybe her grandmother would have some insights on how to get over her nerves.

Lily laughed at herself. After all these years, she *knew* what her grandmother would recommend. Find yourself a man—pronto. Heck, Alma would probably even offer to fix her up. If she were smart, Lily might even take her up on it.

But first, she had a wedding to get through.

Chapter Three

Wedding day minus two. Pete's flight from Miami to Puerto Rico went off without a snag. He smoothly made the connections to catch the noon ferry to the Isla del Oro. Once he was actually aboard, he began to relax. Every arrangement was going like clockwork—a sure sign that he was on the right path. He pushed away any misgivings about his project.

A gorgeous day. The sun gleamed high overhead, and glinting reflections bouncing off the blue waters sent him scrambling for his shades. Pete loved the ocean—any ocean. Funny how little time he spent appreciating the Pacific, so close at hand in San Diego. This was his first time on the Atlantic, and Pete let the rhythm of the waves and the smell of the sea calm some of his nervous energy.

"It's gorgeous, isn't it?" a woman who sounded like she called London home asked.

Pete turned in the direction of the voice and did a double take. A redhead who looked like she was on a photo shoot for some classy magazine was sipping coffee from a Styrofoam cup and watching him. *Gorgeous* didn't only apply to the view, he thought. Was this going to be an even luckier day than it had already been? The breeze ruffled the redhead's long hair. "Sure is," he said.

"I love this part of the world," she said. "Don't get here nearly often enough. So glad Dominic chose to have his wedding here."

Pete shivered from more than just the air.

"Oh, listen to me rattle on." She put her cup in her left hand and held out her right for Pete to shake. "I'm Victoria Laredo. I looked at you and assumed you're either a guest at my brother Dominic's wedding or maybe one of the people who's coming over to work on it. Or maybe both."

Pete shook Victoria Laredo's hand, impressed by the strength of her grip. Of all the luck—he sure hadn't anticipated a conversation with any of Dominic's guests, let alone his sister. Pete resolved to keep his mouth shut. From the way Victoria was chattering, he didn't think she'd notice. "Peter Payne," he said.

"Are you going to the Isla del Oro for Dominic's wedding? I realize there are probably people who have no connection to the wedding on this ferry."

Pete mumbled something about a work assignment.

"Dominic's doing this all up in grand style," Victoria went on. Pete thanked his lucky stars that she didn't question him. "I understand Gwyn wasn't initially thrilled with Dominic's plans, but she's going along with him on this." She chuckled. "I am so glad that my brother met Gwyn. She's been so amazingly good for him. With her around, he's got to back off from being Mr. Perfectionist Workaholic."

Pete did not want to hear any of this. But he couldn't just tell this woman to shut up, and he couldn't abruptly walk away. So he grunted noncommittally, which she seemed to accept as an invitation to go on.

"I have to admit that I was pretty cynical when I first heard that Dominic had found a serious girlfriend. I mean, there have been so many women in his life. But then when I met Gwyn, and I saw for myself how devoted they are to each other... When the two of them are together, it's like electricity arcs and sparks all around them—nearly singeing anyone who comes near."

Pete winced. This was *definitely* not what he wanted to hear. No one had ever talked that way about him and Gwyn together. Well, this woman, attractive as she was, was Laredo's sister. Hardly unbiased. Though she had no reason for telling Pete all these things. She didn't know him from Adam. Pete wondered if she was trying to pick him up. Not that he'd consider being with her, now that he knew who she was...

"Of course, Dominic continues to surprise everyone. He was such a skinny, nerdy kid. And now look at him. All those A-list compilations of bachelors are scrambling to find a worthy replacement."

Humph, Pete muttered to himself. He was available to fill empty A-list bachelor slots. How come no one ever knocked on his door?

"He's been so generous to the whole family since his success. We all either work for him or in other ways share in his new wealth. Growing up, we were always the poorest family everywhere we went. It's made such a difference..." Her eyes took on a dreamy expression.

Just then, a tall, dark man came over to them. "There you are, darling," he said with a slight French accent, kissing Victoria Laredo on the cheek. He was also carrying a cup of coffee.

Victoria looked from one man to the other. "Olivier, I'd like you to meet Peter Payne. He's going over to the Isla del Oro as one of the workers for Dominic's wedding. Never did catch exactly what you do, Pete. Oh, this is my husband."

"Olivier Dulac," the man said, holding out his hand to Pete. "Pleased to meet you, Payne. Has she been chattering your head off?" He turned and looked affectionately at his wife. "And by the way, dear, that's Dominic and *Gwyn*'s wedding. I don't think she'd appreciate your omitting her participation."

"Don't tell her I did," Victoria said, not looking terribly concerned.

Pete had to get away from these two. "Pleasure meeting both of you. The conversation's made the trip very pleasant. Now I'd like to go get myself a cup of that great-smelling coffee."

"We hope we'll see you on the island," Victoria said, waving to him as he made his escape.

Much as he always appreciated the company of beautiful women, Pete could have done without meeting Victoria Laredo—and, especially, hearing what she had to say. He didn't want to hear good things about Gwyn and Dominic together. Finding out about their happiness impinged on his satisfaction with his plot for revenge— and on his justification for even being on the way to the Isla del Oro. After all, Gwyn belonged with *him*. He had to keep his eye on the ball.

The ferry arrived at the Isla del Oro a little after one in the afternoon. He took his place in the queue of wedding guests, wedding workers, and miscellaneous passengers disembarking. As he moved toward land, Pete absorbed the heady early afternoon sunshine, the intensely blue sky, and the palm trees gently swaying—a postcard-worthy welcome. Despite his awareness of his reasons for being in this tropical paradise, he felt himself begin to unwind— and distance himself from any slight doubts Victoria Laredo's words had brought up. Of course, his night of fantastic sex with Nan played a role in his feeling of well-being. He let himself bask in the remembered glow of being with her. Though it had been clear to both of them that theirs was a one-night stand, he'd never forget her or the things she said to him.

But Pete couldn't let himself get too comfortable. He reminded himself that he was not here for fun and games. He had a mission to complete—watching the disruption of a wedding. His primary goal in life at this moment was to be in exactly the right place at the right time to catch Gwyn as her life went into free fall. He checked his watch, then looked up—and froze, nearly causing a mini-collision with the passengers behind him.

There at the foot of the gangplank, watching the arrivals disembark, was the most stunning, breathtaking woman he'd ever seen anywhere. She stood with a clipboard in hand, a goddess in a white linen business suit. He didn't know who she was or fact one about her. Except that her raven hair gleamed with blue and purple lights in the sunshine. Shading her large dark eyes with her hand, the woman looked up—locked eyes with Pete and captured him. He immediately switched his preference for blondes to exotic brunettes. Like a kid on a carousel going for the gold ring, he moved toward her.

* * * * *

The ferry was bringing the floral assistants, the sous-chefs and the other food workers, all of whom had been instructed to look for Lily. Three shuttle vans were waiting in the parking lot to transport the workers to their quarters. She had everyone's name, shuttle, and housing assignment carefully gridded.

And then Lily's eyes clamped on to a tall, sandy-haired man with sea-blue eyes walking toward her in what looked like a trance. She couldn't have said why, but she hoped he was one of her workers. She hoped he was coming with her... She'd already checked off the names of twenty-seven assistants and was waiting for seven more. Two of the twelve-seat shuttles were en route to housing structures — actually dormitories. The remaining workers would return to the resort on the shuttle with the last group. Seven possibilities for him to be one of hers.

The sandy-haired stranger cut through the other passengers and homed in on her. One look and she felt like she'd been caught in an electrical storm with her feet in an iron bucket filled with water. Lily could swear her eyes bugged out like those of a praying mantis on steroids. Her legs could scarcely support the weight of her pulsating pussy — which she swore threatened to reach out octopus tentacles to grab him to her.

Breathe, she reminded herself. Slow down. This man, whom you don't know from Adam, can have no idea of what effect he's having on your internal organs. Not to mention this was the worst possible time for any man to disrupt her personal radar screen.

"Name?" she snapped.

He stared briefly, then said, "Payne, Pete." Two words that fell on her starving ears like a night at La Scala.

Reality check time. She looked at her clipboard and frowned. "I have a Payne, Nate, but he's already checked in." If Payne, Pete wasn't part of the wedding crew, why had he come over to her like all the other workers, including those waiting behind him?

Lily didn't want him to go away, nor did she want to hold up the queue until the matter was settled. "Please step aside, Payne, Pete, while I check the others in. Then we'll see about you."

He did as she asked and watched as she logged in everyone else. Lily hoped the clipboard hid her trembling hands from his scrutiny—and that she could figure out a way to take him with her. Though all her instincts told her she'd be better off if she left him here to take the next ferry back to Puerto Rico.

* * * * *

While Pete waited for the woman in charge, whom he'd mentally named the goddess boss woman, to return her focus to him, he hoped his big shirt and baggy shorts hid his erection. She was obviously shepherding many of his fellow passengers somewhere on shuttle buses belonging to Laredo's Isla del Oro resort, according to the big red letters on the sides of the white vehicles. As much as his scrambled brain could work, Pete realized he'd hit pay dirt on several levels—if only he could persuade Ms. Wonderful to take him on board. In addition to having just fallen into total lust at first sight with her, and wanting to be as close to her as he could get, he'd have an entrée to Laredo's operation.

After she'd finished checking in all the legitimate arrivals, the goddess boss woman turned eyes velvet as a tropical midnight sky to him. "Are you part of the crew here to assist for the Laredo wedding?" she asked, a slight scowl doing nothing to mar the perfection of her face.

Pete nodded.

"I don't understand why your name's not listed." She furrowed her brows as she checked her list again. "Are you food or flowers—or maybe music or photography?" she asked earnestly. "Though people from the last group aren't due to arrive until later…"

For most of his life, Pete had avoided telling lies. Now he found himself in the uncomfortable position of having to maintain a false façade. Having to lie to such a beautiful woman only deepened his discomfort level. But he obviously needed to enlarge the limits of the absolute truth in order to accomplish his mission. "Actually none of the above," he admitted, and then held his breath.

"Oh, maybe I misunderstood," she said, shaking her head. "Are you one of the people working on the Laredo wedding?"

He nodded cryptically.

"I don't understand why your name's not here. What's your assignment?"

To fall in worship before you, he thought. But he merely said, "I'm computer support…"

After an initial flash of recognition, doubt crept into her lovely eyes. "I hadn't been aware that any computer support people would actually be here, on site. I thought you were going to perform all your magic from your various offices."

He smiled. "Figured it's always best to have someone on site as added insurance that things will run smoothly."

"I wish I'd known about this ahead of time."

As she still looked a bit skeptical, Pete figured he'd flash his company ID card, which she took and carefully scrutinized. "Sorry the wires got crossed on this," he said. She handed the ID back to him, and the jolt of electricity from her touch nearly threw him into the water.

Though she didn't look totally convinced, she said, "Well, Payne, I'm glad you're here. I do actually have some concerns I'd like to follow up on. I'll hop on the last shuttle so we can talk, as soon as I've checked in everyone coming on this last ferry." Then she bit her lip. "I didn't know to make a reservation for you anywhere. The island's pretty full. You'll have to stay in a dorm with the food and flower workers."

"That's fine. People call me Pete," he said. She shook his hand, sending another powerful lightning bolt through him. Whew. Pete bit back a grin. He was in. He'd cancel the reservations he'd made at another hotel. Up 'til now, with him so easily gaining access to Laredo's actual site, his plan was working out better than he'd ever imagined.

And the woman of his dreams had just beamed down from somewhere in the stratosphere to be here with him. A woman who'd instantly replaced every other woman he'd ever lusted for. And he didn't know fact one about her. "By the way," he said, keeping his voice casual, "I didn't catch your name."

"It's Tiger. Lily Tiger."

He repeated her name to himself as he climbed on the shuttle and waited for her to join him.

* * * * *

Lily's hormones whirled and swirled in chaotic uproar while she rode back to the resort alongside Pete. Her female instincts had roared to life and were now alive, alert, and threatening to overwhelm her professional stance. Pete had shown her his company ID, so she knew he really was an employee of Fantasia Resorts, Inc. But she hadn't requested any on-site computer support, which was beginning to look like an oversight. Especially because something was not squaring with the off-island shipments of the food and flowers for the wedding. Pete Payne might just be the answer to all her prayers—in more ways than one. Whoa—she had to rein in those thoughts. Work, work, work had to be her total focus until Dominic Laredo and his bride departed for their honeymoon.

She was about to ask him exactly who had told him to come to the Isla del Oro for the wedding when he asked, "Is there anyone else providing computer support here?"

She shook her head. No computer support, no Lily support. "No. And that was an oversight, considering how many people and goods we're bringing to the Isla for this affair. Maybe Dominic's head really is in the clouds. I'm not altogether sure where mine's been."

He grinned and his eyes lit up. Lily wanted to lay her head on his chest, hidden beneath a too-large gauzy white shirt. Pete Payne might be a techno-geek, but he had the slim, rugged physique of an athlete, even a rock climber. Despite the way he hid himself in baggy clothes, she could tell he was really built. His looks and even his name reminded her of a favorite hero from childhood stories— Peter Pan. How happy she'd been to have a version of the name of the Indian princess with far too small a role. Tiger Lily—far braver and more deserving than the insipid Wendy or the troublesome Tinkerbell—should have been

Peter's heroine. Seeing Pete Payne brought back her childhood sense of injustice. Lily would happily fly off with this Peter.

Business first. Lily forcefully reminded herself this was no time to succumb to flights of fancy—or any other kind of flights.

"Sounds like the wedding of the century," he said, his voice setting off a flurry of tingles.

Lily sighed. "After all, Dominic Laredo is a man who knows exactly what he wants—and makes sure it happens."

Pete appeared to shift uncomfortably in his seat. "So I've heard."

She looked at him sharply. "Haven't you met? My understanding is that Dominic makes a point of having at least one direct contact with every employee of Fantasia in their first year."

Now Pete was definitely squirming. Lily made a mental note to investigate his apparent discomfort once they got to her office. "You know us behind-the-scene geeks," Pete said. "We have a well-deserved reputation for avoiding all the usual social situations."

"You don't look like my idea of a behind-the-scene geek," Lily blurted out. She couldn't believe herself—here she was, in the midst of the biggest challenge of her career, and she was going into full flirt mode with some guy she barely knew and had some major doubts about.

"Really? What do I look like your idea of?" he asked softly.

Whoa! Dangerous direction for this conversation to be taking. She looked away, glad they'd be entering the resort compound soon. "I didn't arrange a bed for you in the workers' dorm," she said, "but I guess that would be the best place for you to stay. There must be one or two we haven't yet filled."

"That works for now," Pete said, his eyes telling her he'd be happier wherever he was staying if she'd be there with him.

Lily felt her personal level of heat rise despite the shuttle's strong air conditioning. She made a quick call on her cell phone and arranged for Pete to have quarters. She avoided looking at him or thinking about the man in a cubicle with a bed and... Thank goodness they arrived at the dorms quickly and she'd be distracted by the workers getting settled. All the workers got out of the various vehicles and streamed into the long, low dormitory structures where they'd be staying until after the wedding. Though the dorms were not built to any level of luxury, Dominic Laredo had insisted they be comfortable and unobtrusive, blending into the tropical setting as if nature had planted them there.

Lily directed Pete to the small room she'd arranged for him. She got off the shuttle with him and was planning to wait outside while he dropped his things off. Pete, still carrying the large duffel bag and his laptop, returned in what felt like three seconds. "Lead me to your computers," he said.

Trying to hide her delight at seeing him, Lily asked, "Don't you want to take a few minutes to unpack and freshen up? Why are you carrying all your stuff with you? It really is okay to leave it here. We don't have to be in that much of a rush."

Pete shrugged and gave her his killer grin. "Never can tell when I might need some of the supplies I brought with me, so I might as well just take it all with me. My stuff's not heavy. Unpacking can wait. I want to get familiar with your setup so I can make sure everything goes as smoothly as possible."

She certainly couldn't argue with that. Cripes, he was acting more responsible about keeping the wedding on track than she was. "Follow me," she said.

* * * * *

Lily's office—housed in the same cottage-type structure as the computers that kept the resort humming—was a short walk from the dormitory. As at all the other Fantasia Resorts sites, the on-site tech facilities were a fraction of the machinery located in the central offices. All the offices and resorts were tightly linked to the central office in Dominic's native England.

Pete knew that by now, all the food and flowers ordered from off-island for the wedding were en route to the remote Isla del Oso, which boasted a primitive airport and warehouse and not much else. Even if the misdirection were discovered in time for the goods to be reshipped, the quality of the goods would be so compromised as to render them unusable. The various chefs and florists responsible for the wedding preparations would be stuck with using whatever they could get their hands on locally.

Now that he'd met her, Pete had to admit he felt a twinge of regret for what was about to happen to Lily. She obviously took her job very seriously and would be hurt by the coming fiasco. Like most people who rose in the Fantasia Resorts hierarchy, Lily must be a dedicated employee—if not an out-and-out workaholic. However, none of that would be worth a darn if Laredo got pissed. He'd probably sack Lily.

Well, then Pete and Lily would have that in common—for he was sure this time, Laredo would really fire him. Pete thought back to when he'd gotten into a fistfight with Laredo over Gwyn at her house. After Gwyn had separated them, Pete shouted out his resignation from his job. Laredo insisted they keep their personal differences apart from their professional relationship. Pete remembered how Gwyn's eyes had lit up when Laredo said that, how clear it was, even to Pete, that his once girlfriend was gaga over the guy. But this time, he was sure, Laredo would demand to have Pete's head if he found out what he'd done. And then Gwyn would see Laredo in his true colors. Not for nothing had Laredo chosen the Captain Hook costume for the Halloween party, while Pete was the heroic Peter Pan.

Though Pete now would hate to hurt the innocent Lily, he couldn't let that feeling divert him. Maybe he'd be able to pull off his stunt and still get the fair lady—steal victory from the jaws of defeat like the original Peter Pan. But then he remembered the fair lady he'd first wanted to win by ruining the wedding had been Gwyn. If Lily was now pushing Gwyn from his mind... Did this mean he no longer wanted Gwyn? In which case, why was he here? Confusion joined the mix of emotions swirling around in Pete's head.

For now, he'd have to continue with his initial course of action. Even though he was beginning to suspect this might not take him where he wanted to be. It was too late to change anything.

"Do you want to check out the computer facilities before we talk?" Lily asked, slipping behind her highly polished ebony desk with an amazingly clear surface. Pete took in the décor—a blend of Native American and local arts. He hoped to have time later to look more closely at all the fascinating things displayed—like a ton of owls in various sizes and materials. Why did Lily collect these? What did owls mean to her? He had so many questions to ask. But for now, he had to focus on his role as tech maven.

"In a moment. First, tell me exactly what you're concerned about so I know what to check out immediately."

Lily scowled. "Something seems wrong about the shipments of perishables from our off-island sources," she said.

Yeah, he thought, that about summarized what should be happening right about now. Lily certainly was up to the minute in the various details of the preparations. Time for him to start acting. He felt a pang of discomfort for what he was about to say and do. "Perishables?"

"Yes. Primarily food and flowers," Lily said. "Though part of our basic operational philosophy is to rely primarily on indigenous goods to give the resort an organic, natural feel, for the wedding Dominic wants to go farther afield. He's brought in chefs from Paris and New York and wants to have several different gourmet menus."

"Sounds a bit over the top," Pete said.

Lily smiled. "Who'd imagine anything else for Dominic Laredo's wedding? He's of course done the same for flowers—wanting the different venues decorated in totally different styles. That's why we've had to bring in so many workers. And then of course with all the guests and people who'd previously made reservations on the island..."

"How many people are we talking about here?" Pete asked, wanting to extend the time of their talk as much as he wanted to postpone discovery of what he'd done.

"Well, there are three hundred guests. That number alone is far more than we can accommodate here at Fantasia." Lily raised her eyebrows and riffled through some papers from a file she took from a drawer.

"Fortunately, all the other hotel owners on the island are cooperating and have made their rooms available to the wedding guests. Then we have the six chefs, five florists from Hollywood and New York, three photographers and three videographers, also from Hollywood, and fifty-seven assistants. Plus the head chef and chief florist."

Pete chuckled and shook his head. "Sounds more like a movie production than a wedding."

Lily nodded her agreement. "Just imagine what it would have been like if Dominic didn't want to keep the affair intimate." She frowned and began rubbing the back of her neck.

"What's wrong?" Pete asked, springing to his feet. "Do you have a pain in your neck?"

"Lots of them," Lily said ruefully, rubbing the sore spot. Pete wanted his fingers to be where hers were.

Suddenly her discomfort was the most important thing in the world to him. Anything or anyone that threatened Lily became his target. He had to help her—and he knew how. Pete took a deep breath. Okay, so he was overreacting. Being near her jolted all his responses into the stratosphere. He'd need to keep his voice sounding normal so she wouldn't regard him as some sort of maniacal stalker.

"I've got great hands for massage," he said, "or so I've been told." He held his large hands up in front of her. "Why don't I give you a neck rub? I bet I'll be able to help you unknot those tight muscles...and lots more..." His voice trailed off huskily, and he switched to the language of his eyes.

Please, please, please, let me touch you. Please know that I'm a wonderful person and not a crazed lunatic. Let my fingers linger over your most vulnerable and secret places...he begged her silently.

Pete had never been much for imagination, but now he could practically feel what it would be like to caress Lily. Her skin would be soft yet electric to his touch. His penis, already at a state of high alert from her nearness, sprang to aching fullness. He stifled a moan as he shifted his legs, trying to find a comfortable position. But he knew there was only one possible position for him right now — near Lily, over Lily, under Lily, in Lily. Any way he could manage it. Moving in and out of Lily, driving her wild with pleasure. Kissing her deeply, his mouth and teeth the advance team in his journey of exploration. Her lush breasts crushed against his chest, their hearts hammering together in rhythm. God, he ached to suckle at those breasts, nibbling at her nipples as they grew stiff with her excitement.

She'd be so wet for him. Her glistening pink folds would peek out at him from the dark, curly hair guarding her mysterious entrance. Pete's cock began to throb at the thought of her slick, sweet wetness welcoming him deep into her.

He'd take her first right on her big, clear desk, then rolling around on the carpeted floor. Plunge into her and open up a whole new universe for them both.

Okay, so she'd be on top. After all, he didn't want to hurt her back, pounding into her on these hard places. Didn't ever want to hurt her in any way. Wanted to love away her pain and troubles. Now. Here. His cock was ready to explode.

A multitude of emotions flashed by so quickly in Lily's eyes, that Pete's head began to spin. Did she think he was being too aggressive, just out to get his hands on her any way he could? Did she know how much he wanted to touch her, how he craved the contact? Didn't she know how hard he was for her, how he'd never before in his life wanted another woman so much? Did she know he'd give his left nut to put a smile on her face?

By the look in her eyes—shock, confusion, and maybe, just maybe a shred of desire—Pete knew he was about to strike out—big time. He bit his lip, wishing he could take back his words. No. What he wished was that Lily would just say yes.

* * * * *

Talk about temptation. Lily's whole body thrummed with irrational desire for this man she barely knew, and her breathing sounded ragged to her ears. What she wanted most in the world at this moment was Pete's big hands, his long fingers, kneading away the tight spots, loosening her, soothing away all her frustrations—and transporting her to a whole new plane.

It took very little imagination to know how hot and arousing his hands on her would be. She'd always loved long fingers. On her neck, on her back, on her breasts, kneading the tender skin right where her thigh met her hungry, hungry pussy... Don't go there, she admonished herself. His fingers, her pussy. Her panties were soaked with her desire for this man. With his long fingers, he could touch all the places in her pussy that were weak with longing. She'd ride his fingers, in her and on her.

Right now. Right here, in her office. On her desk. She and Pete. Their loving would forever banish the image of Bert Stone shagging her assistant in this very place, replace it with the energy of the two of them pleasuring each other...

Despite Pete's loose clothing and the way he kept trying to wriggle into less obvious positions, Lily'd spied his nearly constant erection. She wanted to grind herself against him, feel that rod up close and personal with her mound. Cripes, she was nearly drooling with her desire for him. She swallowed hard, and wished she could take his cock in her mouth.

And then she'd take him inside her moist and ready pussy. She'd put her hands on his amazing ass and go for the ride of her life.

Yikes! Lily breathed deep and used every drop of her willpower to get a grip. That was all she needed now — to let this man she had serious work to accomplish with get his gorgeous hands on her horny body. She looked around the room wildly. Her glance snagged Ollie Owl, guardian of her desk. Thank God for Ollie. Ollie silently brought Lily back to reality — and wisdom.

Lily had to put a lid on her galloping hormones — immediately. Show those suckers who was boss.

Luckily, before she could answer Pete—and tell him to bug off in her frostiest, lady boss voice—the phone's shrill ring demanded attention.

"I need to get that," she said, trying to keep her voice professional and level as she reached across her desk.

"Let your machine pick it up," Pete said quietly. His eyes were big with longing, and his shorts tented out. Lily averted her eyes. After all, how much could a woman take?

Man, she wanted to ignore the phone's summons. She'd let him massage her—knowing in her gut where that would lead.

But her businesswoman's instincts refused to put up the white flag of surrender. The ringing stopped before she could answer or the machine kicked in. "Probably not important," Pete said.

Even if that was the case, the ringing phone clearly signaled her responsibilities. Two heartbeats later when it began to ring again, she turned away from Pete and picked up.

Carmen Lopez, her assistant. "Thank God I found you!" Lily frowned. Carmen was usually Ms. Calm, Cool, and Collected.

"What's up?"

"The shipment of food and flowers from off-island. It's gone."

"Gone? Gone where? How?"

"Gone as in disappeared." Carmen's voice hit a very high note by the time she got to the last word.

Lily scowled into the phone, feeling the first stabs of a major headache strike right above her eyebrows. "What do you mean, gone?" she asked, keeping her voice soft. The calculator part of her mind clicked into motion and began running the figures of what those shipments cost. And how much it would cost to try to come up with some alternatives Dominic Laredo would go for at this late date. Shit! Fuck! Damn! Here—in living color—was the disaster she'd been dreading and expecting.

"All the special orders of food and flowers. The shipment was supposed to arrive here an hour ago for the wedding. It's not here."

"Where is it?" Maybe all wasn't lost.

Carmen exhaled hard. "I've spoken with the dispatchers and trackers. Bottom line—no one knows where the plane is."

Lily sat back hard in her chair. The missing shipment would screw up Dominic Laredo's wedding—and coincidentally ruin her life. She felt sick. Dominic had personally arranged and authorized all the orders of food and flowers for his guest chefs and florists. All she'd had to do was make sure she delivered everything to the chefs and florists in a safe and timely fashion.

She'd done everything right at her end—so why had the shipment gone down the tubes? Later, she'd have to sort it all out. Right now, her workload had just quadrupled. "I'll be right on it," she snapped to Carmen. "Meet me at my office in ten minutes with every scrap of information you have."

She hung up and looked at Pete, who'd heard every word of her end of the conversation. Wait a minute—Pete was a computer hotshot from one of Fantasia's offices. He'd be able to help. She managed to suppress any thought of acting on her carnal desires now and turned her energy completely to the business at hand. She hoped.

"What's wrong?" he asked, looking a bit wary. But still sporting a full erection, Lily couldn't help noticing. Desire flared. She couldn't give in. She licked her lips, bit them, and consigned her inner horny woman to limbo.

Lily repeated the outline of the situation in the fewest words required. "So as I see it," she concluded, "we have to find where the stuff has gone and get it back here—in time for the wedding preparations." She began to pace. "Cripes, the florists and the chefs should be dealing with the delivery of the stuff in a short time. Well, if we can manage to transport the goods here even later today, they can pull all-nighters getting everything set. God knows Dominic is paying them royally."

Lily stopped in her pacing and glanced at Pete. For a split second, she suspected that he looked very strange—almost ambivalent—about the situation at hand. But that must have been her overwrought imagination at work.

"How can I help?" Pete asked.

She eyed him. "You're tech support, thank goodness. Pete, let's get you set up and see if you can find just where our shipment has disappeared to. Then we'll know how to proceed."

Pete looked as if he was about to say something when Carmen arrived. Lily introduced him to Carmen as a tech support expert from the San Diego office and instructed her to get him set up on the computer. Something about San Diego and the wedding flashed through Lily's mind. But she didn't have time to chase the thought now.

First thing, she had to get on the phone and see if she could come up with a Plan B, in case the worst happened and they could not find the goods. She picked up Ollie Owl, and mouthed a silent meditation. Then she speed dialed several crucial numbers.

As Pete followed Carmen out of Lily's office, he turned and made visual contact with her for a brief moment. Was that regret she saw in his eyes? She turned away to focus on her phone calls. She couldn't let herself think about the look in Pete's eyes—or his persistent erection—now.

Chapter Four

Pete, grateful for Carmen's silence, followed her into the office next to Lily's. He could have sworn that, à la Pinocchio, he felt his nose growing longer than his cock every time he lied to Lily. Wrong story. No one could see any visible sign of his lies on his face, he was sure. He figured his cock would subside eventually—especially as he was banished to the other office, away from Lily.

Of course, it didn't take long for Pete to learn as much as he needed from Carmen to log onto the computer and have access to all the information he needed locally. All the Fantasia Resorts, Inc. offices were linked and in constant communication. He was on home ground here.

The much bigger problem was to figure out what to do next. Because he knew *exactly* where all the food and flowers Dominic had ordered for the wedding were now. The plane had landed an hour before on the Isla del Oso, where the crates of expensive goods were off-loaded and left to rot in a primitive warehouse. Nonetheless, Pete had to go through the motions of an unnecessary search. He logged on and watched the screen spring to life, then he went into a fog. Man, was he ever screwed.

Even if he were able to somehow reverse the process and initiate the immediate transport of the goods to the Isla del Oro, there was no way to get the goods here in a timely, usable fashion. And, worst of all, there was no way he could carry off any sort of attempt at a salvage operation without revealing to Lily that he'd been the culprit behind the plot. According to Fantasia procedures, he'd have to get authorization from Lily to order the reshipment of the goods on the private plane. She'd first have to contact the person who currently had the authority for dispatching the shipment, who was...Pete. At the least, she'd have to wonder why he was going through so many steps to transfer authority from himself to himself.

The last thing on earth he wanted right now was to do anything that would sabotage the possibility of his maybe having a relationship with Lily. Relationship. Lily. She was where his desires were now. Just a short time with that woman had him thinking words like this in a way that none of his previous involvements had. And they hadn't yet done anything more than shake hands. Well, that and a lot of fantasizing on his part. He winced, suddenly having more insight into what went wrong between Gwyn and him. Nan's words about his unfulfilled potential came back to haunt him.

He'd known Lily for just a short time, but it was enough to realize his feelings for her were more special than he'd ever experienced before. But he'd have to be blind not to see what her career meant to her. The air around Lily crackled with her ambition. And Dominic Laredo did not promote anyone who wasn't the cream of the cream.

All of which put Pete out of his zone of comfort. His scheme was working out perfectly—and everything he now wanted for his life was headed down the tubes. If it hadn't been for getting pissed at Gwyn and plotting revenge, he'd never have been here on the Isla del Oro, never have met Lily Tiger. And how was he repaying Gwyn? By ruining her wedding. Not to mention what his plot would do to Lily's career plans.

There had to be some way out before the full disaster came to life. Pete pounded his head with his fist. He just had to think.

The moment he'd met Lily, all thoughts of being with Gwyn evaporated from Pete's heart, mind, and libido. Why had he ever imagined Gwyn to be so essential to his sex life? He'd thought he was in love with her—had even proposed marriage to her. Sort of. He hadn't really been serious—she'd known it, and he had to admit, so had he. Now, after just a short earth-shaking time with Lily Tiger, every other woman he'd ever known faded into a distant haze. Lily was the only woman he wanted in his arms— and in his life. Everyone else—even Gwyn, even Nan, even his third-grade teacher, Miss Petrie, wonderful as they'd been at the time—had only been practice.

Talk about being a dead man. Pete had no illusions about how Lily would react when she found out what he'd done. And it was inevitable as the sun rising in the east that she would find out. Lily was far too clever to be fooled for long—especially after she and Laredo put their heads together. Not to mention how much Pete hated lying to her. Back to that.

Pete took a long swallow from a water bottle Lily had supplied. The realization that he could just come clean to Lily flashed before him. He frowned. Here was where their short acquaintance complicated life. Though he was sure she'd be furious, he really couldn't predict exactly what Lily would do. Part of that was not knowing how she felt about him as a man—a big question mark.

On one hand, maybe she'd so admire him for his honesty and courage in coming forth and accepting responsibility that she'd forgive him for screwing up the biggest deal of her career. She'd take him into her luscious arms, run her fingers through his hair, kiss him deeply, and press her body against the erection her presence near him produced. An erection not unlike the one he was getting this very moment just thinking about her.

Yeah, right. Talk about Pete developing an overheated imagination. Lily would probably be so filled with rage, she'd throw him off the island and order him to have no further contact with her. Ever.

His erection collapsed.

Though he'd like to consider himself a courageous sort, a risk taker like his role model Peter Pan, there was too much at stake here. Lily's reaction was too unpredictable and too important for him to chance it. He reluctantly decided to brazen things out with the scheme he was mired in.

The phone on his desk rang and he picked up. "Payne."

"Pete," Lily said. Her voice sounded happy to him. "Just wanted to check to see if you have everything you need."

"I would if you were here with me," he said.

"This is a business call," she snapped.

Pete winced. No sense pissing her off before he absolutely had to.

"Sorry. But being here on this beautiful tropical island, I'm beginning to feel work is way overrated."

"Wrong time for you to take that attitude. I want information about that shipment within the hour."

"I'll get it to you."

"Buzz me if you need anything—and, especially, if you find out anything definite sooner."

"Ten-four," he said, trying to sound as lighthearted as he would have if he had a clear conscience. The phone clicked in his ear.

Within moments, Pete had up-to-the-minute tracking information on the goods. Damn, he was good—at screwing things up. The cargo plane that had deposited the goods on the Isla del Oso was by now heading north somewhere above South America.

Maybe, just maybe, he could contact the pilot of that plane and have him return to the Isla del Oso to pick up the goods. He tracked the plane and found it was still in Chile—grounded at a small airport north of Santiago with engine problems. Would take at least a day for repairs.

Another nail in the coffin.

Even if he could dispatch a plane to the Isla del Oso immediately, the goods, after hours in a warehouse with no refrigeration, would be too far gone to be of any use. And it was far too late to try to reconstruct the original order and reship from New York, where the smaller shipments from Paris, Hollywood, and other world centers had been assembled.

Pete paced in the room and wished he had a dartboard. Throwing darts always helped him focus and think creatively. His eye fell on a small marble owl he could swear was glaring at him malevolently. Owls represented wisdom, a commodity he felt to be in short supply. Owls didn't belong in the tropics. He'd ask Lily why she had one guarding her computer room. That is, if he ever had another chance to ask Lily about anything personal again.

* * * * *

After formulating a basic plan B—namely, getting hold of the best quality local goods and workers she could—Lily put down the phone and took a few moments to regroup. Despite the heart-racing thrill of meeting Pete today, this was probably the worst day of her life. The best and the worst—talk about a schizophrenic situation. Had Aunt Dolores ever had days like this? Lily appealed to Ollie the Owl for grounding and guidance. But for once, Ollie came up short.

Lily now had dozens of high-maintenance workers lolling around the island with nothing to do but take a very highly paid holiday. Dominic Laredo and his bride would be arriving early the next morning to check in with her. Lily frowned, trying to grasp the elusive thought that kept escaping just beyond where she could take in its dimension. Something Dominic had said about his fiancée?

Lily knew her boss expected the morning's meeting to be a routine check. Though Lily had always found Dominic to be the best and most supportive of bosses, she did not relish having to tell him about this snafu. Especially not the day before his wedding.

Well, at least she wasn't alone. Pete was doing some tech magic to see what he could learn. Maybe the goods were only slightly delayed after all. She'd go to the computer room to find out the latest. She could, of course, just pick up the phone...

Lily stood in the doorway for several moments and watched Pete at work. He sat fixated on the screen, his clear blue eyes wide under his furrowed brow. Just looking at him, she felt herself grow moist with desire and the need to press her legs together—preferably around him. She appealed to all her guardian owls to keep her focused.

"How's it going?"

"Oh, Lily. Has it been an hour already?"

"Not quite. But I figured I'd get a progress report. So, tell me some good news."

He exhaled what sounded almost like a sigh. "I wish I could. But from what's shaping up here, doesn't look like we have any good news."

She frowned and went over to the computer, standing behind him so she could look at the screen. Wrong move. Being this close to him, she could scarcely keep her hands to herself.

"Maybe you should pull over a chair," Pete said.

He was being more sensible than she. Lily got a chair from the nearby conference table and slid it over next to Pete. Lily willed herself to concentrate on the problem—and on where her career would go if she didn't fix this mess. "You'd better tell me what's going on."

Now Pete did sigh, and Lily braced herself. "Right now, I'm trying to track the shipment of the goods you're waiting for."

"It should be pretty straightforward to find them, shouldn't it?" Lily knew that Dominic Laredo's state-of-the-art technology should make short work of finding the errant plane.

"It should be," Pete said. "But for some reason, the transport is not showing up when I key in the numbers that are supposed to track it."

This did not sound good. "I don't understand," she said, feeling dim and not being sure if this was a reflection of her business situation, her lack of tech savvy, her nearness to Pete—or all three.

Pete shook his head. "When I key in the tracking numbers, the message I get is that they're invalid."

"Okay. So, what are you going to do next?"

"I'm going to go to step one of the process—when the orders were placed. Then I'll track every step to see exactly when things got messed up."

"How long do you think it'll take?"

Pete shrugged. "Depends what I find."

"Much as I want to know what went wrong, even more I want to know how to make it right." Was it her imagination, or did Pete look slightly green?

"In this situation, I don't think we can start working on a solution until we really know where the initial error came in."

"I don't agree. I need some hard data from you right now. I do have a Plan B, and I'll need to get it operational if the shipment is really gone beyond all hope." She got up to head back to her office.

"I should have some more solid information for you within the half hour." Pete turned to the screen, then back to Lily. "Uh, it's probably the wrong time to ask, and all, but I'm going to go for it. Lily, can I take you out for dinner tonight?"

His voice sounded charmingly unsure, and he looked so damned hot. But she couldn't let him distract her. "You're right. It's the wrong time to ask," she said, her voice dripping icicles, she hoped.

Pete's face fell. Lily didn't want to scare him off permanently—just get him to back off until they got through the crisis.

"Look, Pete," she said, her voice now softer. "I don't know what dinner tonight or any other meal is going to be—until I get the wedding stuff squared away. Might be some peanut butter crackers and a Diet Coke out of the vending machines."

"Sounds good to me," he said.

How could she resist someone who was willing to eat out of machines to be with her? A warning voice told her to keep things in very low gear. "Let's see. If we can both arrange to take time out for a meal tonight and we're in reasonable shape for the wedding, maybe we can eat together." She eyed him a moment. "Which would not be a date, understood?"

He grinned, and she could have sworn he was wagging his tail like a big overgrown puppy. Oh, she didn't want to go there. Didn't want to think about his tail, about his amazing butt... Lily splashed mental cold water over herself.

"Pete," she said, looking at her watch, "Dominic's going to be here first thing tomorrow morning to check in. We must have the situation resolved before then, so we can tell him all is going as it should be."

"I'm doing my best," Pete said softly.

Lily went back to her office. At least her gut had been warning of disaster for the past few days. Though she wasn't happy to know she'd been right in her forebodings, she wasn't totally unprepared.

"Okay, Winnie," she said to another of her guardians, a wooden owl who did double duty as a bookend on the console near her desk. "It's time to reach out to the community. I'm going to list all possible suppliers close at hand, then I'll phone them to see what quantity of goods they can get to us immediately."

In her gut, she knew the original shipment was irretrievably gone. Thank goodness part of Dominic Laredo's work ethic—and hers—was to actively pursue and maintain excellent relations with everyone in the community. Dominic Laredo's generosity characterized his relationships, even with his competitors, who would all be on alert now to help her implement Plan B.

Lily had just finished listing all her contacts when her phone rang.

"I have good news and bad news," Pete said.

"Give me the good news first," Lily replied, hoping it would outweigh the bad.

He sighed. "I know where the food and flowers are."

Lily stared at the phone for a moment, wondering why Pete was stretching out the suspense. "Give it up, Pete, now," she said, standing up. If Pete knew where the goods were, they could get them and eliminate the need for her to make all the calls to suppliers.

"They're on the Isla del Oso."

"The Isla del *Oso*?" she echoed. "The Island of the Bear?"

"Yes. That's the place."

"Never heard of it," she said, wondering why Pete sounded so subdued. This really was good news, wasn't it? "But Pete, it's great that you found out where everything is so quickly. Now we can get everything sent back here."

She heard Pete sigh again. "Not so fast."

"Why not?"

"The Isla del Oso is way off the coast of Chile. It's at least an eight-hour flight from here. And the goods are already there, under less than ideal conditions. No refrigeration. By the time I could send a plane there and get them reloaded to ship here, they'd be sludge."

"Shit!" Lily exploded. "Shit, shit, shit!"

"I agree."

"Sorry," she said. "*Shit* is not a professional response."

"But accurate for the situation at hand. Lily, what's next?"

"Looks like I'll have to put Plan B into action. How the hell could this have happened?"

After a long pause, Pete said, "The two places are only one keystroke apart on the computer..."

His voice sounded strained to her, but maybe that was just a reflection of her taut nerves. She realized he was probably correct in his guess as to the technical, stupid typo reason for the snafu. The names of the two islands were nearly identical. Knowing that wasn't worth a darn. All that mattered was fixing the mess. For now, she needed to get to work to salvage what she could. Pronto.

"How can I help with Plan B?" he asked.

"Come in here, and you can help me keep track of what we're going to do. I want to be the one who phones all my contacts, but then we'll have to figure out how we're going to pick up replacement goods and get them to the appropriate workers."

By the time Lily realized Pete had hung up, he was by her side, looking hotter than ever.

* * * * *

Pete once again offered to massage Lily's neck and shoulders.

"Look, I'm happy to have your support here, but you have to stop offering me massages. Not professional," she snapped.

"I'm good, but I'm an amateur," Pete said, holding his hands out to her.

"Last warning. You keep trying to distract me, and you're out of here." She picked up the phone and scowled at him.

Pete backed off.

"I'll give you the list of the people whose crews will help us. Please check the numbers against the various jobs we have, so we'll know how to allocate people. I'll phone everyone and tell them we're going to Plan B. Then I'll phone the suppliers."

She made her own list as she ran down her list of phone numbers.

With the two of them working, they got through the necessary phone calls and basic paperwork in less than an hour.

"What can I do to help next?" Pete asked, hoping there'd be something. He both wanted to help her and maybe, just maybe, begin to redeem himself.

Lily smiled at Pete, getting his heartbeat up and his cock alert. "I'm afraid that once we get moving, most of the way you'll be able to help will be pretty low tech."

He held up his underused hands. "I'm a man of many talents. Good for way more than massage, though I'm world-class at that."

"If you're serious about helping me, you won't say that word again to me today," she said, blushing ever so slightly. If he hadn't been studying her so intently, he'd have missed seeing the faint color rise to her cheeks.

Pete, wondering, hoping, that he was the source of her agitation, enjoyed her blush. Maybe, maybe if he made himself very useful, he'd be able to survive this situation and come out on the other side with Lily in his life. But first he needed to convince her he really wanted to help, and stop screwing around. "But seriously," he said, "I want to do whatever I possibly can to help you wrap things up here as early as possible. Maybe the evening can turn out to be more than just a vending machine snack together…"

She made a face. "*Au contraire*, my friend. We might have to pull an all-nighter to make this work—and I don't mean a fun and games one."

"Any all-nighter I pull with you definitely does not fall into the category of work," Pete said. Then seeing her eyes snap, added, "I'll be good. Scout's honor." He held up his right hand.

"Just wait and see what I have planned for you. I'll be amazed if you don't bail."

"I'll be with you 'til the end," he said, his hand quickly crossing his heart.

Her phone rang before she could respond. She turned her attention to a conversation with someone named Pierre who evidently had a good supply of chickens available.

Pete began to feel restless, just sitting in the office and listening to Lily's part of her phone conversations. After she'd made two more calls, she said, "Maybe you can go with the crew to pick up some of the goods I've located."

Thrilled to finally have some physical activity to help release his growing nervous energy, Pete sprang up. "I'm ready. So how's it all shaping up?"

Lily pursed her lips. "Looks like we'll be able to get more than enough food and flowers for our needs. Problem is, they won't be the ones Dominic's imported chefs and florists specified. You see, Dominic's plan was to combine native foods and flowers with special ones from everywhere else. Now we'll just be stuck with whatever we can get our hands on locally."

"Will that really be so bad?" he asked, hoping to hear her say it wouldn't.

"Not bad, per se. Just different than what Dominic has ordered up for the day."

Pete winced. Everyone who worked for Fantasia Resorts and most of the western world knew that Dominic Laredo was notorious for wanting his specifications carried out to the nth degree. Laredo often said his attention to detail was the secret behind his success. Pete hated being reminded again exactly what he was doing to beautiful Lily's career with his plot for revenge—and perhaps to any possibility of them ever being together for more than work.

* * * * *

Lily didn't know for sure if she'd be able to salvage the situation, but she'd sure as hell go down trying her damnedest. It felt good to be active, taking steps to some sort of solution. Heck, she'd cook and decorate with flowers all night if that's what it took.

Pete seemed willing to help her, to do any of the grunt work she'd direct him to. If there was one saving grace to this whole fiasco, it was that she'd met him. Lily would swear that Winnie the Wise was winking at her—though Ollie Owl kept scowling.

Everyone Lily spoke to agreed to contribute food, flowers, and energy to the Laredo wedding. By the time she'd gone through her lists for the third time, Lily had located enough food and flowers to supply three large weddings more than adequately.

Lily would send Pete with the crew gathering food, Carmen with the flower gatherers. The two crews would bring their loads to the various staging areas. Lily herself would work on organizing the chefs, the florists, and all the assistants. She knew the imported help would not be happy with the changes of materials and with now having to work more directly with the native contingent. But in the final analysis, that was too bad. After all, being hand-picked to cater and decorate for Dominic Laredo's wedding was a coup for anyone's career. Still, Lily knew she'd have to deal with many large egos—hardly a first for her. Well, Dominic Laredo paid top dollar—for which he expected one hundred and ten percent. That included everyone rolling with the punches.

Pete, a gleam in his eye, started to say something. Lily had agreed to meet him for an informal dinner—not a date. He looked like he was going to press for more. Lily wanted him to…

A knock on the door ended her brief flirtation with irresponsibility.

"Come in," she called out. Carmen Lopez entered, looked at her boss, then at Pete, then at both of them together, and said, "I can come back later."

Shit, Lily thought. The chemistry between her and Pete was thick enough for other people to see. She couldn't give in to that. She shook her head. "No need. We're all leaving. I want both of you to check back with me in an hour about what's going on with your crews—sooner if there's any problems."

Pete saluted her. She watched them both leave, then set to work.

First on her list was to deal with the fancy chefs and see what kind of foods they'd have to replace. Hoping physical activity would distract her from her growing desire to just throw herself at Pete, Lily walked the short distance to the banquet facilities where her chefs were drinking coffee and gossiping. She was about to make a nasty comment when she reminded herself how hard they'd be working—soon.

Thank goodness her French, which had gotten pretty rusty, sufficed for communication with Henri Bertrand, the first chef she spoke to.

"But this is impossible!" he protested when Lily brought him up to date on the changes.

"Our meal plans include custom Scottish beef, the finest Beluga caviar, Italian Prosciutto ham, Alaskan salmon, and cheeses from the provinces of France. Not to mention the truffles. *Sacre bleu*, the truffles." The large man grew very red in the face and nearly began to weep at the thought of the truffles.

Lily knew how he felt. "All gone," she mourned with him.

He threw his hands open in a gesture of helplessness before disaster.

Lily drew herself up straight and tall. She couldn't let herself or anyone connected with the wedding fall into negative thinking. With as few words as she could, she outlined her plan—and humbly requested Monsieur Bertrand's expertise to help save the day.

That was the right approach. With a sigh, he gathered his colleagues and explained the situation in surprisingly good English. After conferring loudly and passionately, they decided the best approach would be to ensure quantity using the highest quality goods they could get their hands on in time. Which was exactly what Lily's initial plan had been. They agreed Lily would be in charge of contacting local suppliers; she didn't need to tell them she'd already done so. The chefs swore that they would perform their magic on the ingredients she would provide.

With the faint stirrings of hope that they just might salvage the situation, Lily left the chefs to their conferring. She promised they'd have their ingredients with all due speed.

* * * * *

When Pete agreed to help the resort crew pick up food for the wedding, he hadn't realized this would include getting up close and personal with over a hundred live chickens and a goat. Before this, he'd thought food came canned or wrapped in plastic from supermarkets. Now he quickly had to adjust to the reality that, in the next day or so, the noisy creatures his crew was transporting would be transformed into the food for wedding guests. Pete fervently hoped that Lily would not expect him to be any more involved with the transition than delivering the goods to the pros.

On the other hand, Pete had to do whatever he could that would give him a shot at being with Lily once the wedding was over.

So he couldn't just opt out after the deliveries were over, and everyone had to report for their next assignment. "Choose your detail," a harried crew boss barked at Pete.

"What are my choices?" Pete asked, hoping he could find some work that didn't involve food prep.

The grizzled man looked at him dubiously. "You ain't never done this before, right?"

"Right you are, my friend." Pete hoped this would earn him an instant dismissal. Instead it got him a spot on the chicken feather-plucking team. Pete was directed to a large kitchen where huge piles of dead chickens filled the air with a pungent scent he'd never before experienced.

"Watch José," the boss said when Pete protested ignorance of the process.

José, a large swarthy man with bulging muscles, must have been a champion plucker. After watching him denude three birds, Pete was told he knew enough to get started.

By early evening, Pete had learned more about defeathering poultry than he'd ever thought he could. He also had to admit he was the slowest man on the team. For sure he was the man with the most muscle aches. He hoped every tug of a feather, every blister and ache, would take him a step further toward making him worthy of the fair Lily. Only thoughts of her sustained him.

During the first hour, he'd inspired himself with erotic images of the possible uses of chicken feathers. He imagined taking one of the larger, whiter feathers and lightly running it over Lily's face, then down to her magnificent breasts. Was she ticklish? He'd have to find out for sure. Checking that no one from the crew was watching him, Pete ran the feather over the skin on the inside of his forearm in a test. His skin erupted in instant goose bumps, not to mention what his cock erupted into. Pete stifled a groan. He wished he could be running the feather down between Lily's breasts right now. He shifted as his groin grew tighter in his usual reaction to thoughts of her.

Pete would lightly trace her whole body with the tip of the feather, then follow its course with his lips. He'd play with Lily's pubic hair, relishing the contrast between her tight black curls and the stark white of the feather. Or perhaps Lily was one of those chicks who shaved away her pussy hair. Pete had once gone out with a woman who'd surprised him with a shaved pussy... What was her name? Her pussy hadn't been exactly hairless. More like she had a friggin' Mohawk...dyed purple.

Pete's cock throbbed, and he once again gave thanks for his loose clothes. He couldn't wait to find out if Lily really was hairless down there, ticklish, so many mysteries... His gut told him that she probably had a healthy bush of real hair. He'd bury his face in her bush, smelling her, tasting her... He licked his lips, imagining her pussy right there in front of him and nearly whimpered with need.

Reality check time. He hoped he'd have the chance to find out anything about her. But once she knew his role in forcing them all to slave away today…and all his lies to her…

Though his fantasies helped while away the first hour, the unrelieved tedium of the work soon killed off his imagination and his erection. Pete swore he'd never eat another drumstick.

The odiousness of his task was almost enough to kill all his appetites—almost. But despite his new aversion to fowl, by ten o'clock that night he was more than ready to eat anything else. His hunger-enfeebled brain began to come up with schemes for getting excused long enough to find some form of non-chicken food. He figured by this time, Lily must have eaten whatever dinner she'd been able to get. Disappointment over the lost chance to be with her flooded over him.

But then, like a heavenly vision, his angel of mercy arrived in the smelly, chicken-dominated kitchen. Lily. She hadn't forgotten their plan or abandoned him. Pete wiped his greasy, feather-coated fingers on the makeshift apron tied around his waist. He suspected Lily was stifling a laugh when she looked at him, but he didn't care. As long as she had come to rescue him.

"What are you, Big Bird?" she quipped.

"More like the Bird Man of Alcatraz," he said, eating her up with his eyes. He wanted to be alone and naked with her—almost badly enough to postpone the satisfaction of his rumbling belly.

"Well, Bird Man. I'm here to spring you," she said. "Unless you have a burning desire to continue with your, uh, bird defeathering operations."

"Even if I did, which I don't, I'd give it all up to be with you." He looked hard at her and hoped he hadn't just leapt to an unwarranted assumption. She was being warmer to him than she'd been that afternoon, when she'd been pretty frosty. He had to move carefully with her, but not too carefully. No woman had ever tied him up in so many knots before. "That is, I assume…"

"You assume correctly, Pete. You're coming with me now." She turned to the crew chief and continued speaking. "José, it looks like everything's under control here. You'll be able to finish without Pete, won't you?"

"We can spare him. He done good for a beginner. Now the pros can finish up." José turned away from her to return to his own chicken plucking. Though dressing chickens had never been a skill Pete aspired to develop, he could still admire those who'd elevated it to an art.

"Are you really done for the night?" Pete asked Lily when they'd walked outside. Maybe she was a sadist, dragging him off to some other hard labor.

"I shouldn't be. But realistically, there's nothing else I can do until morning," Lily said, stifling a yawn. "I'm astonished by how many people are pitching in to help. So I'm taking a break for dinner, then I'll have to check a few things before signing off for the night. And tomorrow's going to be a really long day. But I figured you probably hadn't eaten yet either, and you don't know your way around the island—outside of the chicken pluckers' central and the suppliers' places. Also, I think at some point I mentioned sharing a trip to the vending machines with you."

"As long as I don't have to eat chicken, I'll be happy." Hell, as long as he was with her he was happy. But then he got a whiff of himself. Being out in the fresh air didn't do much to take away the smell of chicken and sweat. "Uh, Lily, I really need to clean up before I think about eating."

"Sounds like a plan. Pete, I'll take you back to your dorm room."

"Actually, I left all my stuff at your office."

Her eyes lit up. "Great. Let's collect your gear. Then you can shower at my place. Follow me to my car."

"Unless you're driving an old clunker convertible, I stink too much to get in," he warned as they walked the short distance to where her red late-model BMW — definitely not a clunker by any stretch of the imagination — was parked.

"I cannot get in there. How about you tell me where you live, and I'll walk? Or you drive slow and I jog fast right behind you?"

She looked at him. "You really do smell rank."

"I warned you."

She went around to her trunk and took out a black trash bag. Pete hoped this wasn't a symbol of where she thought he belonged. After she opened the door, she covered the passenger seat with the plastic. "You can sit here. We'll keep the windows open, and I'll spray with air freshener tomorrow."

"Not too flattering."

"Get in," she said, walking around to the driver's side and getting in.

He did. She drove back to the resort complex. They stopped in her office so he could collect his things. As long as they were there, she picked up a file. Then they walked the short distance to her cottage. Though Pete was dying to touch her, he was just too grubby. But once he hit the shower and started feeling human again...

* * * * *

The nightmare day was finally giving way to a more hopeful night. Lily grinned as she congratulated herself on getting wedding plans—not the original ones, but alternatives that might just work—well in progress. Now that the day was drawing to a close, she'd let herself relax some of the iron control she'd kept over her feelings all day. She was getting Pete to her place. Not that she thought the last would be difficult to accomplish, but she was never one to take anything for granted when it came to men. She still wasn't sure what she was going to do with him once she had him home. But she was beginning to think they both deserved a break after the kind of day they'd put in. Especially as it looked as if they were going to pull off a save. And Pete had turned out to be a good sport—showing up as tech support and throwing himself into the hard physical work needed.

Grubby and smelly as Pete was, Lily could barely keep her hands off him. Even the odors of chicken feather residue and his labor-induced sweat hit her like a sizzling aphrodisiac. Self-control, she reminded herself. You're a professional. This is a work situation.

Maybe bringing him home for a shower hadn't been her best idea, but she couldn't back down now.

"There's liquid soap and shampoo in the shower," Lily told him, pointing to the glass-encased stall of her gleaming white bathroom. A skylight and large uncovered window brought the lush outdoors in. Tonight the moon and a million or so stars were pouring forth their light. She handed him a plush white Egyptian cotton terry towel. She knew she should leave him alone in the bathroom, but she couldn't make herself walk away.

"I've never wanted a shower so badly before," he said. "Uh, Lily, can you steer me to a laundromat? No way I can wear these clothes again or even pack them with my other things."

"Take them off. I'll throw them in my washer."

"That's really nice..."

"Hey, you smelled good before you started helping me out."

"Why shucks, ma'am, I didn't think you noticed," he said, going into shy cowboy mode complete with western drawl.

She swatted him with a towel. "Cut the b.s. and get into the shower. I'm too hungry to wait much longer."

He mock bowed, then rose and pulled off his shirt in one fluid move. Balling it up, he handed the white cotton, still warm from his body, to Lily. She tried not to stare — but damn, he had an amazing body. Great pecs, little brown nipples she longed to tongue, and a line of sandy brown hair leading down from his navel to the top of his low-rider shorts...to his...

He had his hands poised at the top of his fly, watching her now for permission.

"I guess you want some privacy," Lily said, wondering at his awkwardness and starting to feel awkward herself, mixed with her lust and her renewed energy.

"I don't usually drop my drawers unless I'm sure it's okay with…" he leered, looking at her from under half-lidded eyes.

Lily steeled herself not to blush. "Come on, dude. Hand them over so I can get the wash going."

He turned around, then watched her over his shoulder.

"For Pete's sake," she said. "I grew up with four brothers. I've seen naked men all my life. No big deal." She could hear her grandmother Alma saying, "Right."

Pete grinned, then gazed at her for a moment. With his back still to her, he unzipped his fly. All her senses jumped to attention at the sound. With a slight but amazingly provocative wiggle of his tush, he pulled down his shorts. Her underpants grew moist and she clenched the muscles of her lower belly, telling them to behave. Standing in his Super Hero boxers, Pete tossed the shorts to her over his shoulder.

"What about your boxers?" she asked, trying to sound cool which required her to swallow hard several times. "Don't they need to be washed too?"

"Yeah." He stepped out of them, giving her an eyeful of his high, tight butt as he bent over to pick them up. Lily clutched his clothes tightly to keep her hands occupied.

He turned back around. "I guess it's not polite to keep tossing my wardrobe to you," he said, grinning.

Lily swallowed hard. He was huge and classically hung. Did the guy ever not have an erection? Her pussy grew moister in response to that question.

"Oh, wow," she said, her voice as detached and casual as she could make it. "Is that the Incredible Hulk?"

He raised an eyebrow. "Are you referring to the boxers or my love muscle?"

His love muscle? Lily rolled her eyes. "Why, to the boxers, of course."

"Oh," Pete said, looking wistful. "Yeah, got it on your first guess," he said.

"Do you usually wear Super Hero boxers?"

Pete shook his head. "I also have cartoon characters."

"Cool." Lily feasted her eyes on his gorgeous body. Pete was too glorious not to enjoy—though she might stop short of labeling his penis an incredible hulk. She'd need more than visual evidence to decide if that would be truth in advertising… Lily mentally slapped herself and repeated the *Behave* mantra she'd been struggling with since meeting Pete. "You'd better get that shower so we can go eat," she said reluctantly. "I'll get the washer going."

"Right," Pete said, stepping into the stall and turning on the water full force. Then he stuck his head out. "How about joining me? There's lots of room." He waggled his eyebrows.

That's all she'd have to do. Get naked and get in the shower with him. Lily's hormones stepped up their race through her bloodstream, and her panties turned into a sodden mess. Coolly turning him down rated with swimming in the Bermuda Triangle as far as challenges went. But she could do it. "You really think there's enough room for me, you, and your inflated…ego?"

"Yeah," he said, evidently not one to get shot down by a put-down. "Also good for water conservation. You know, the two of us getting clean, saving resources…"

She rolled her eyes again. Not the most professional response, but it beat the hell out of jumping in with him. "You're wasting water now, Pete. Let's get on with it. I'll throw your clothes in the wash, you get rid of the chicken smell. After we eat, I still have some things I need to check on…"

"Can't blame a guy for trying," he said before finally closing the door.

Trying was right. It was more than trying keeping him at arm's length. Lily bit her lip and took the clothes to her washer. Granted they smelled disgusting. So why did she want to clutch them to her heart and inhale deeply? The scent was nine parts chicken and one part Pete, but that was enough to turn her on. Hell, at this point sharing the oxygen in the house with the man was enough to turn her on.

So where was owl wisdom when she needed it? Lily got the washer going and tossed in Pete's clothes. Then she figured she'd calmly walk to her bedroom office and go over one of her lists while she waited for Pete…

When she passed the bathroom, the door was open. She stepped in to close the door so that Pete wouldn't get a draft when he stepped out of the shower. The bathroom was filled with steam, Pete whistling tunelessly. She called his name, just to let him know she was closing the door. But between the water flowing and his whistling, he must not have been able to hear her.

Against her better judgment, Lily stood for a moment and watched him through the distortion of the frosted glass. Then she snapped out of it. What the hell was she doing? She should walk out now. Heck, she shouldn't have been here in the first place. If she was feeling domestic enough to do the laundry, she should go to the kitchen, see what she could come up with in the way of food. Not to mention those lists she wanted to check...

But then he began to sing—not quite on tune. Actually way off. The way he messed up the song got to her on a whole different level than he would have if he'd been at perfect pitch. He surprised her with his choice—the old Beatles' classic, "Yesterday".

She could have left if he'd sung anything else, or at least she told herself that. But "Yesterday" was her favorite song in the world for when she felt blue. How could she leave now? She frowned. Why was he singing a sad song? Did he really feel so caught up in helping her with the wedding that he'd caught her mood? After all, the problems weren't of his making, and his job wasn't directly on the line like hers was. He was here, working above and beyond the call of duty to make things good. She'd be sure to point that out to Dominic. Why, then, did he feel his life had been so much easier yesterday—before he'd met her? Did it have something to do with her, or was she being paranoid? Could she ask him—now?

He sounded so sad. She wanted to comfort him. Ignoring the voices of Aunt Dolores and several owls, Lily stepped out of her white linen suit and her silk underwear and laid them aside. Without saying a word, she opened the door and popped into the shower with Pete.

Pete had his back to her. The moment she opened the door he gasped, turning to her like a plant to the sun. And then his eyes began to gleam with wonder, and he stopped singing. Everything about him told her how happy he was to see her. She could tell by his smile, his eyes, and his erection, which seemed to grow even longer and fuller.

"Why were you singing 'Yesterday'?" she asked over the steady flow of the water.

He shrugged. "Because I know the words?"

"You certainly don't know the tune." Now that she was in the shower with him, she felt happy—but also less sure of herself. Her questions and concerns of just moments before dissipated like the mist around them.

"You don't like my singing?"

Lily snorted. "I hope it's okay for me to join you in here," she said as the hot water streamed down her face and body.

He laughed. "Okay? Lily, you've just made a great shower perfect," he said, reaching out for her with his hands full of her lavender-scented liquid soap. "Not to mention that we're doing our bit for conservation. Want me to lather you?"

"Sounds great," she said. "But first, tell me why you sounded so sad."

"Did I sound sad?" he asked, looking at her wistfully.

"Yes," she said.

He shook his head. "How could I possibly be sad with you here with me? It's just a song, Lily. Let me lather you."

She tried to shake free her feeling that despite his words, he definitely felt blue. Between what they'd managed to pull off today and her rising tide of lust, she was feeling almost euphoric—and she wanted him to share that. "Okay. I'll soap you too."

"You first," he said. "Turn around, I'll start with your back."

When she turned around, he whispered, "Hold your hair up off your neck."

Grabbing a handful of hair, she formed a loose topknot and closed her eyes as Pete began to massage the back of her neck with the soap. Yeah, he really had magic hands. As he stroked her, Lily began to release the concrete knot she'd been carrying around in her shoulders. She moaned softly, and he stopped. "Did I hurt you?"

"Oh, no." She stepped back towards him a fraction of an inch, just enough to feel his hard cock nudge her cheek. Another small step and he had the full length of his erection pressed against her back. She leaned back and rubbed against him. Even better than his massage.

Pete abandoned his massage and drew her closer to him. "I thought you were going to soap me," she said lightly.

"Something's come between us," Pete whispered, nibbling her shoulders and back. "Later for the soaping. Turn around, Lily. I want to be in you, now."

Lily licked her lips. She was ready, and she felt like she'd been waiting forever. She wanted him—hard and deep. "I'm here," she said, her voice low and husky.

Pete growled and pulled her to him. Pete ran his hands down her sides, and despite the warmth of the water, Lily shivered. She imagined that they were standing under a warm waterfall out on a mountaintop, the only two people in the world. Pete kissed her, a deep probing joining of their souls, surrounded by the scent of lavender soap and the quiet hiss of the water streaming around them. Lily met his tongue with her own, wanting more than anything to know every inch of this man, who he was, what he dreamed of. He broke the kiss and backed away from her, leaning against the tiled wall. He gazed at her, his eyes large and deep blue with longing. With all the steam and the mist, Lily felt like she was in a dream with him—and yet touching the most intense reality of her life when she stroked him with her trembling fingertips. She moved ever closer to him, pinning him against the wall.

"Oh, Lily," Pete moaned. "If only I'd known you before..."

What was he talking about? Why did he still sound so sad? Why was he bringing any thought of unhappiness into the closeness they were sharing?

"Promise me you won't ever regret anything that happens between us tonight," he whispered.

Normally far too cautious to make any such promises without major discussion and analysis, Lily would have said anything at this moment if it would bring her what she craved—the satisfaction of the desire she'd burned with since she first locked eyes with Pete. "I promise," she said, not thinking beyond the moment. She stroked his face, then ran her lips from his mouth down, down, pausing to kiss his tiny brown nipples on her path to his throbbing cock.

Pete tasted delicious to her, like chocolate and flowers and lavender and...love. Lily quivered. She wasn't going to let her mind go there. She was going to really taste him, to get to know the flavor of every inch of Pete. Lily knelt before him, cupping his balls in her hands, savoring their heft and texture as the water showered around her. She nestled her face into the joining of his legs, then took his enormous cock into her eager mouth.

Pete gasped, moaned her name, and ran his fingers through her hair.

Lily almost laughed with the pleasure of having him in her mouth. Pete smelled like soap and water, like light and joy—the chicken feathers and sweat a distant memory. Running her tongue over every ridge of his cock, Lily thrilled to the pleasure she was giving this man. For tonight, she wanted to taste him, touch him, feel him, smell him in every way possible. Hell, she was so hungry for him, maybe she'd invent some new ways for them to be together.

Pete's cock grew and throbbed, filling her mouth with his excitement. Lily would have been content to go on sucking and licking him for hours, but Pete took her by the head and pulled away. She looked up at him, wondering why he'd stopped her.

"I want to pleasure you too, before I come," he said, drawing her up. "Keep on like that, and I'll come in about three seconds..."

She shook her head. "Pete, don't you think I was enjoying that?" she asked.

"Come here, my darling Lily," he said, pulling her close in his arms. He had to bend his knees to get to the right height for his cock to connect with her pussy. Lily leaned her arms against the wall and spread her legs in welcome for Pete. The moment his cock came into contact with her aching slit, she thought she'd explode through the ceiling of the shower like a rocket-propelled missile. He felt like silky velvet over steel as he thrust into her hot, wet sheath. Lily let go of the wall and hung on to Pete's shoulders for dear life.

Wanting to maximize their contact, she arched against him, pressing him so hard into the wall that he'd have tile imprints on his back for days.

Lily longed to clutch on to Pete's delicious ass, but that was impossible in their position. She reached up and dug her nails deep into his shoulders as he drove himself into her, arching his hips in such a way that her clit vibrated with the stimulation of his continuing friction. Pleasure radiated from her pussy. Oh Lord, what the man did to her.

Pete was clutching her to him. As he did magic with his cock, his fingers were playing with her anal crack, bringing her new pleasure from a source she'd never before known about. While her pussy muscles massaged his cock, stroking him with her smooth pink sheath, she pressed her anus against his probing fingers, marveling at how much pleasure she was feeling in his arms.

All the while he was kissing her, murmuring her name like she was a goddess and he her humblest supplicant. Lily thought her heart would burst with the mix of sensations and feelings Pete was bringing out in her. Her whole body hummed with pleasure—from her toes to her teeth, to her hair, long slipped free from the topknot. Her heart soared in rhythm with his, caught up in their own song, making it impossible to know where the boundary between them lay.

She was flying up a mountain, climbing him, climbing with him, flying over the earth far into the heavens. Her cry of release rose from the depths of her being, echoed from the walls around them. Pete let loose an incoherent oath, then tore himself from her just as he began to ejaculate in great warm throbs.

Lily hated being wrenched from him like that, just when she wanted to be close to him. But then what little scrap of her mind was still working flickered a message—no protection. She'd never before lost herself like that with a man before. Thank goodness Pete had been rational at the moment of peak experience, even if she hadn't.

Pete Payne was far too dangerous for her. He scared her, but she wasn't about to run.

Were those tears in his eyes, or was it the moisture of the shower. "You came before me," he said tenderly, holding her to him now.

"I did," she said, wondering what he was getting at.

He drew away from her for a moment. She wanted to cuddle against him under the falling water, but she could see the question burning in his eyes. "Did I give you pleasure?" he asked.

Her gut told her this was not a casual question. She closed her eyes for a moment, a wave of remembered sensation washing over her. "Oh, God, yes," she said. "Oh, definitely." She wanted to nuzzle his neck forever. The two of them could turn into prunes from the water, and she wouldn't care.

"Thank you," he said, searing her lips with a kiss.

* * * * *

For Pete, being with Lily was like his best Christmas and his worst dental appointment rolled in one. From the moment she'd stepped into the shower—and yeah, she had abundant curly black hair all around her beautiful pussy—Pete felt like he'd found the genie and gotten all three of his wishes.

She was everything he'd dreamed of. And she came before him. He satisfied her, and God knew she satisfied him in every way possible. But...but...he knew what lay ahead for the two of them. Her bleak disappointment, the betrayal she'd feel once she knew what he'd done...

He wasn't going to ruin this once-in-a-lifetime night for either of them by letting the reality of the situation bring them down. He'd shut down the part of him waiting for the dentist's verdict. He already knew what the verdict was going to be.

Like a condemned man who was about to have his last dinner, Pete would thoroughly savor each moment with Lily. He'd make it special for her. And he'd give her the night of her life.

Chapter Five

Eventually the water began to cool, which did little to put a damper on the two of them. They started soaping each other, then realized that they'd be there all night as each nook and cranny demanded attention. Which might not be a bad thing, but other appetites also called. So after lots of playing and making many bubbles, Lily and Pete actually finished washing before they got out of the shower.

Every movement between them, including the mutual toweling off, was a total sensuous experience. But Lily began to emotionally back away from the intensity of their lovemaking as soon as they stepped out of the shower. No doubt it was great and more special than any other time in her life, but it couldn't have been as mind-blowing as she'd thought, could it? After all, in the long run, the most they could be to each other was a work-induced one-night stand, right?

There she was, analyzing again. Well, she didn't have to reach any conclusions tonight, which was great. Her mind must have been worth about ten cents at the moment. She put on red cotton shorts and a white tank top, which played up her olive complexion and dark eyes and hair. Pete scrambled into jeans and a T-shirt advertising a neighborhood burrito stand back in San Diego. Her mind snagged on the name San Diego again. What the heck was it about that city that kept nagging at her? Maybe it would come to her later. When she looked questioningly at the T-shirt, he shrugged and said, "It was free."

"I guess you've earned dinner. Hell, we both have," she said to Pete, once again feeling shy with him. "I see you like burritos. We don't have much Mexican food here on the island, but we can go out to…"

"Let's just stay in and eat whatever you have here," Pete said, taking her by the hands. "I don't want to go out anywhere."

Lily made a face. "I'm not a very good cook, and there's not a lot in my freezer."

"I don't have much of an appetite after all," Pete said. "That is for food."

Lily swallowed hard. She didn't have much of an appetite for food either, but she wanted to establish some distance between them. Otherwise they'd both burn up from spontaneous combustion before morning—and Dominic Laredo was due in to get updated on the damn wedding.

"I might have some frozen dinners we can nuke," Lily said, taking her hands from Pete's and heading off to check out her freezer.

"Want me to help you?" he asked.

"That's okay," she said. "I'll just be a few minutes."

* * * * *

Pete watched Lily walk into her kitchen. Though he'd have preferred to be with her every minute he could, he wanted to respect her unspoken desire for some space at this moment.

Never before had he experienced anything with any woman like he had with Lily. She blew the top of his head off and had him floating in some unknown, distant stratosphere.

How could he have fucked things up so royally? After Lily's initial coolness, she'd turned into flame and fire, singeing him with her heat. If only he'd known what he was throwing away when he came up with his stupid plan...

By this time tomorrow, he'd be history as far as Lily went. Laredo would arrive on the Isla del Oro in the morning, and Pete would probably be on the first ferry out. That is, if Laredo didn't have him thrown into some local jail, where he'd rot away like the food sent to the Isla del Oso. People would forget him. Lily would never see him again. And his life would be over. Or if Laredo somehow could be convinced not to throw him into jail, maybe he should consider joining a monastery or something, pretend his future celibate life was his choice.

Well, at least they'd have tonight. He'd have to make the best of it. Memories of being with Lily — and regrets at what he was going to lose — would probably have to last him for the next fifty or sixty years.

Lily, looking like a princess goddess, now came back into the living room and offered him a drink. "Red or white?" she asked, holding up two wine bottles.

His usual drink was beer, but he'd drink what she did. "What are you having?"

"The white's chilled and probably goes better with whatever I've got squirreled away in the freezer," she said, holding out one of the bottles for his inspection.

"The white it is," he said, willing to drink hemlock to be with her.

She went back into the kitchen and returned moments later with two wineglasses filled with light amber liquid.

She handed him one and held the other up. "Let's toast."

"To us," he said, clinking his glass to hers.

Her smile lit up her face and tugged at his soul. "To the successful completion of our roles in the Laredo wedding." She clinked glasses again and seemed not to notice as he choked.

* * * * *

Lily took a healthy swallow of her Chardonnay. "So Pete, wanna come into the kitchen and help get dinner together — or are you a domestic-phobe?"

He drank a bit of the wine, made a face, and put down his glass. "Domestic-phobe? Can't say I've ever heard that term before."

"Oh, you know. One of those guys who can't boil water and turns pale at the thought of nuking a frozen dinner in the microwave."

"After I just spent hundreds of hours plucking feathers from chickens?" He repeated the hand motion he'd learned that day. "Methinks the lady sounds a bit, what's the word, *chauvinistic*?" Pete asked, waggling his eyebrows. "Especially as you admitted to not being well-accomplished domestically."

"Ouch. I may not win any Martha Stewart awards, but I'm capable of nuking a frozen dinner—and boiling water," Lily said. "And I did manage to get your clothes washed."

"Well, if being able to do those three things saves a guy from being a domestic-phobe, I'm safe. Can nuke," he said, kissing her lightly on the lips, "boil," another kiss, "and launder." A last kiss. This time she couldn't stop herself from kissing him back. Though she wanted more, Lily pulled back.

"So come into the kitchen, keep me company," Lily said. "This way you'll get your say as to which of the frozen dinners we eat."

"Your wish is my command," Pete said. He took his wine with him.

Lily's kitchen, the least utilized room in her house and her life, contained all the basic necessities—and that was about it. Fridge, stove, oven, microwave, dishwasher. Everything was modern, coordinated, and barely touched. Lily opened the freezer door and thanked her lucky stars that she'd done a large shopping somewhere in the recent past. Maybe the time Grandma Alma called her up and bawled her out for eating all her meals in restaurants and treating her home like a hotel room. When it came to domestic arts, Lily definitely followed the Aunt Dolores model. Usually that worked for Lily. But today she was glad she had something to feed Pete. Heck, they even had a choice between pepperoni or cheese and extra veggies.

Lily indicated her freezer shelves. "Let's see. There's pizza, pizza, and, oh, more pizza. Also looks like I've got some mac and cheese, not highly recommended, I must admit. And there are veggie burgers, tofu Florentine, pound cake, whipped topping, and rocky road ice cream."

"Did I ever tell you how much I like pizza?" Pete asked, his lips twitching in amusement.

"Hey, if you're hungry enough…"

He laughed, put down his glass, and took her hands. "I really do like pizza. Actually I love pizza. It's my favorite food—has all the essential food groups. Dairy, meat, veggies, and Lily."

"I'm not a food group," she said.

"You should be. You'd be at the top of my pyramid. Essential: To be healthy, wealthy, wise, and sane, I must have Lily every day."

She waved him away, preferring not to have to deal with any thoughts of the future just yet, thank you very much. "You're either nuts or crazed from starvation. So, Pete, what kind of pizza do you prefer?"

"I'm a pepperoni man," he said.

"Pepperoni it is," she said, pulling a colorful box out of the freezer. She squinted at the box. "We need to preheat the oven, then bake the darn thing for half an hour. You okay to wait that long?"

He nodded. She turned on the oven, put the pizza on a cookie sheet, popped it in the oven, and turned on the timer. "Let's go wait in the living room 'til it's done."

Lily sat down on her blue and white striped loveseat, and Pete followed. Loveseat. She'd never before thought about what a great name that was for a piece of furniture. Pete's thigh pressed against hers, sending a new wave of lust right to her clit. She didn't want to go there, didn't want to get on the roller coaster of desire again. Hell, the sex in the shower should have been enough. She should have moved away, but couldn't bring herself to break the contact. Food and drink, she thought, distracting herself. Food and drink. She took another sip of her wine, wondered if she should put out some crackers or something so it didn't just go to her head—the way it was doing.

"I'm curious," Pete said. "Where'd you get frozen pizza on this tropical island? After today I figured you all usually eat fresh chicken, barbecued goat, and those native vegetables."

She shrugged. "Some people do go native for their entire lifestyle. For the rest of us, there's a full-service supermarket on the island. Like a lot of other people here for long-term assignments, I started missing some of the comforts of home after a few months. So I go stock up at the Good Deal—source for Doritos, Oreos, and Sara Lee. All the leading brands you'd want under a tropical sky."

"So where's home for you, Lily?"

Good question. Where was home for her? "That's complicated," Lily said.

"I've got all night."

She could somehow believe he'd listen to her if she chose to spend all the hours from now 'til morning talking. But she could think of other activities... Talking would do for now. As for the rest, the night lay tantalizingly before them. "The short answer is Oklahoma, Tulsa. At least that's where I spent my formative years—and I think that's what you mean. Of course, home now is the Isla del Oro."

"I'd like to hear more about your complicated answer," Pete said.

"Not tonight," she said. "Not after all the stuff that went on today. I promise I'll tell you everything some other time — after we get through this wedding."

Pete looked down at the floor. Was she taking too much for granted, assuming he'd be around to talk to after the wedding? She was about to try to ask him when he changed the subject. "I notice you have a lot of owls around. Do you collect them, or what?"

Okay. She was up for taking the easy way out in conversations tonight too. "Yeah, I do." She stood up and crossed over to the shelves where she had much of her collection displayed. "The owl is my special animal."

"Your special animal?" he asked.

"My Cherokee grandmother, Alma, taught me everyone has a special animal — one with qualities that resonate for her. A person needs to discover what her special animal is and then invite that animal into her life. One way to do that is to surround herself with images."

"Fascinating," Pete said. "How did you find the owl is your animal?"

Lily grinned. "I've always loved owls, since I was too little to say their names. They came to me in dreams and told me they'd always be special to me, try to take care of me."

"Let's see. Owls represent wisdom, right?"

She nodded. "Though these days, I'm feeling less than wise. But I'm doing all the talking. What about you, Pete?"

"There's not much to tell. Born and raised in San Diego, still live there. Mother, father, two older brothers. Been playing with computers since I was little. Now I work with them."

Lily chuckled. "Talk about the condensed version... I want to hear way more. But Pete, I have to tell you. Ever since I met you, there's something in the back of my mind about San Diego... Every time you mention that city, I try to catch a thought that keeps eluding me."

The timer went off before he could respond. With the two of them bustling in the kitchen, they had the pizza sliced and ready to serve in moments. They sat down and made short work of the pie.

"You're still hungry, aren't you?" Lily asked. Pete had wolfed down five slices of the pizza to her three and looked like he could have eaten another whole pie by himself.

"I wouldn't say no to dessert," he said.

"That's easy to do." She started coffee brewing then nuked some pound cake. When it was warm, she spooned on rocky road ice cream and some whipped topping. Pete's eyes lit up.

"You look like a dessert man," she said. He grinned and dug in. When he'd had two more helpings and two cups of coffee, Pete offered to help Lily clear up.

"Thanks," she said. "I guess you're not such a domestic-phobe after all."

He looked wistful. "Things I learned the hard way from my last girlfriend."

Did he still miss her, whoever she'd been? Lily felt a pang of resentment toward the unknown woman Pete was evidently still thinking about. "I'd like to hear about her," she said softly.

"For another time also," he said.

So, he was thinking about seeing her again. Her heart soared.

Pete had a funny gleam in his eye. "Say, Lily, you got any more of that whipped topping?"

"Yeah," she said. "You still hungry?"

He just grinned. "Bring it here."

* * * * *

Pete loved whipped topping and he thought Lily was delicious. So why not bring the two together?

They were both standing at the counter in Lily's kitchen. Eyeing her, he took the lid off the plastic tub, stuck his right index finger into the cool white confection, removed a dollop, and spread it over Lily's lips. He then proceeded to lick the topping slowly off her lips.

Lily's eyes, large as saucers, reflected surprise and—pleasure, he was sure.

"What's that?" Lily asked. "What are you doing?"

"I'm improving the taste of the topping," he said.

"That's what I thought. Let me try," Lily said, imitating Pete's movements. She sucked the sweet white confection off Pete's lips, then licked her own. "Mmm," she said.

God, she was so delicious. Pete wanted to pick her up in his arms and carry her off to her bedroom, caveman style. He wished he had his own secret island to take her off to, a place where he could hide her away from anyone or anything that would come between them.

"I liked that, what you did with the whipped topping," Lily said. "But how'd you think of doing it?"

Pete shrugged. No point mentioning that he'd learned this from Gwyn, who'd tried lots of creative games with food. "One of my fantasies. That's part of something I've always wanted to do." Okay, another lie. But even he knew talking about a former girlfriend would not be a good idea at this sensitive moment.

Lily slitted her eyes at him and put her hands on her hips. "Part? Pete, I want to hear the rest of your fantasy. Or fantasies. Tell. Now."

"I'd much rather show," he said, sweeping her up in his arms. "Let's take this to your bed," he said, swirling her around.

"Right," she said. "Only don't forget the whipped topping."

He scooted down so she could pick up the tub then ran with her to her bedroom.

Lily's bed was covered in white silk and several hundred throw pillows. Owls, both in pictures and as figures gracing shelves, watched benignly over the room. Lush orchids, perfuming the air with their heady scent, rose from a sleek crystal vase. A wooden ceiling fan whirred quietly. A gentle breeze wafted into the room through slightly open French doors. A desk and a file cabinet in one corner looked well-used.

Pete carefully deposited Lily on her bed. She reached up and pulled him down next to her. "Too many pillows," she muttered, pushing several out of her way to move closer to him. "And I need to move my bed owls to a more comfortable place." These she put on her night table.

"Too many clothes," he responded, starting to divest himself of his.

"Agreed." She slipped out of her shorts and shirt, then lay before him glowing in the evening light.

Pete caught his breath. Lily was almost too beautiful to touch, but he wasn't going to let that stop him. Not tonight. He was going to make tonight life-altering spectacular—for both of them. He'd start by being totally real with her as to who he was. Okay, totally real with her except for not admitting to the big lie of why he was there. And when she booted him out of her life tomorrow, he'd have tonight to remember forever—to keep him warm when he was a miserable, little old man mumbling to himself as he rocked in his solitary chair on the porch of the nursing home.

He took her in his arms and began to kiss her. She melted into him, her body a perfect fit. Pete wanted to touch every inch of her, memorize every nuance of her flesh with his fingertips and what remained of his brain. He started to run his hands all over her. Then some inner voice called out two words: Slow down. Slow down. Of course. He may not have forever, but he sure as hell had all night. He didn't intend to waste a moment of that sleeping. Now he would touch her with the careful reverence of an artist sculpting his masterpiece. Slowly. Savoring every point of contact. The erection that was a permanent fixture when he was near her grew. But even his cock needed to slow down for tonight.

Lily ran her foot along his leg, doing some slow reconnaissance of her own. She wiggled her toes against his erection, letting him know she knew it was there, tacitly agreeing with him that they'd keep things slow…for now.

"Pete," she murmured, breaking their kiss. "Where's that whipped topping?"

"Why?" he asked. "Getting hungry?"

"Oh, yeah. And I just got inspired on how to use the topping to satisfy me."

He grinned and reached for the plastic tub.

* * * * *

Had Lily really believed she could distance herself from Pete tonight? All her thoughts of resisting him and acting professional had as much substance as whipped topping left out in the sun.

To think she'd had the whipped topping in her freezer forever and never realized what possibilities it offered. Lily positioned Pete just where she wanted him, lying on his back, then stuck her finger in the tub and laid a dollop of white stuff on each of Pete's nipples, which she hadn't paid nearly enough attention to before. Pete's nipples stiffened at the first touch of the cold white dessert. His gorgeous cock beckoned to her, throbbing in time to the thrum of her clit. But for now, she was going to go for some deferred gratification. Soon, soon, she promised her hungry pussy, she'd offer a home to that amazing cock.

Lily straddled Pete, being careful to limit contact with his cock to some casual brushes and flickers that had him groaning and her nearly ready to abandon any delaying tactics. First things first. She lowered herself and slowly began to lick the topping off Pete's nipple. He startled so at the first contact of her tongue to the hard little nub that she thought they'd both end up in a heap on the floor. She pressed down harder on him so the dark curly hair of her mound was tickling his rock-hard shaft. Yeah.

Pete was twitching with need, and Lily gloried in her power over this magnificent specimen of man. Disciplining herself to continue with great deliberation, Lily sucked the topping off his second nipple. Pete whimpered something incomprehensible.

"Is that good?" she murmured.

"Oh, God," he whispered.

"See what you started with your fantasies?" she asked, already anticipating how nuts what she was going to do next would make him.

When she'd licked both nipples clean, Lily shifted slightly. Pete raised his head to see where she was going. "Just be patient," she said, reaching her hand into the tub. The whipped topping felt wonderfully cold and smooth to her fingers, but even ice couldn't have cooled her down now. Not when she was going to slather his cock with the whipped topping. She felt like a combination gourmet cook and sculptor.

Pete gasped when she stroked on the first layer. His penis contracted momentarily, then sprang to full glory, larger then ever. Lily smacked her lips and lowered herself so she was eye level with his shaft. Pete had his legs spread so that she could fit between them, but that wasn't what she wanted. She wanted to feel his leg between hers, to rub her aching clit against his hard thigh—and she put herself in exactly the right spot to do it.

Pete's head fell back against the pillows as she began to lick the topping from his cock. He moaned monumentally. Lily moved her hips against his thigh in rhythm to her lapping up of the whipped topping—which had never tasted better before. Idly she wondered if she should send this serving tip to the firm that handled advertising for the manufacturer. Could open up whole new marketing possibilities. Pete was now moving his own hips, becoming a living lollipop that fed her hunger with his own. Her tongue traveled the length and circumference of his penis, thoroughly licking off every drop of the topping. But, oh dear, she must have been sloppy when she'd coated him, for she found some topping had dripped down to his balls. Well, she couldn't let them be neglected.

Shifting position slightly, Lily proceeded to tongue his delicious balls, fingering his cock so it wouldn't get lonely. When she'd licked both turgid sacs clean of the dessert topping, she put her lips back around his erection. By now her clit was starting to feel very happy from the friction of Pete's thigh rubbing her just right. She really liked what was happening there and widened her legs so more of it could happen. Ooh, she could feel a come brewing—and she definitely wanted to help it along. Eating Pete was feeding her excitement in a way she'd never before experienced. She deepened her embrace, savoring his feel and taste as he filled her mouth.

There it was. There it was. She was coming on his leg. She could feel her fluids began to spurt and her muscles spasm around his friendly thigh. With his penis full in her mouth, Lily cried out—as much as she could. Pete stiffened and then groaned. "Lily, I'm going to come in your mouth unless you get off. If it's not okay, please get off."

Lily had never swallowed a lover's cum before. But now she wanted Pete to come in her mouth. She didn't want to have to leave him, not at this moment. In response to his frantic whispers, she buried her head lower in his groin and held on. "I'm coming," he called. And he was. And he did.

With the first spurts of Pete's fluids, Lily was almost startled—despite his clear announcement of what was happening. And then she allowed herself to taste him—salty, almost bitter, in piquant contrast to the sweet topping she'd swallowed just before. Lily savored every last drop of Pete's cum, stroking his side to let him know she was cool with what was happening, licking and sucking.

At last Pete sighed and collapsed. Lily tongued his penis one final time to make sure she'd gotten everything. Then she slowly lifted herself from Pete and lay down next to him.

But not for long. She'd thought Pete was dozing. He surprised her by lifting up on one shoulder and grinning at her, his eyes filled with what looked like adoration. "Turn about's fair play," he murmured.

She raised her eyebrows. "You may not have noticed, but I came—once again, before you."

He leered at her. "Your first of many times to come—as the night is young."

She laughed dryly. "You've got my attention."

"Oh, I want more than that. How about we start with having you on your back." His words trailed off in a kiss of such tenderness that Lily felt her eyes well up with tears. When Pete withdrew, she lay back down among her pillows, and he covered her with his body. Lily drank in his warmth and gentle hardness. She wanted to explore his wondrous body for hours, days. But she knew that every expedition of discovery would give way to lovemaking, because he was totally irresistible, and she had years of need to fill.

Pete skimmed over her face with his fingertips and his lips, trailing heat and light everywhere he touched. Lily wrapped her arms around him and was about to do the same with her legs when he began to lower himself along her body. He suckled her breasts, laving one nipple with infinite slowness while his fingers paid homage to the other. New hunger and desire flared in Lily's deepest core, and she arched herself to him. He continued with his deliberate provocation, leaving her wet and whimpering for fulfillment. With a sigh, he left her breasts and began to nibble his way down to where she wanted him. Lily could not stop her legs from twitching or her fingers from raking Pete's back.

"I'm about ready for dessert," Pete murmured, his hot breath puffing tantalizingly on her aching slit. "Where've you got that white stuff?"

Lily pointed in the direction of the nightstand. Pete reached his long arm over and came back with a huge handful. "I want my pussy à la mode tonight," he said, coating her with the cold white topping. Lily nearly jumped to the ceiling when its coldness touched her sizzling pink folds. She chuckled as she pictured the topping melting, releasing her pent-up steam to the ceiling. Now she wished she had a mirror up there so she could watch Pete bring her to ecstasy. Instead, she closed her eyes and visualized.

* * * * *

Once Pete had Lily exactly where and how he wanted her, he treated himself to the unique gourmet dessert she was. God, she was gorgeous—her black hair curling and poking invitingly through the sweet white covering. Talk about scrumptious. Lily didn't need any added flavoring to make his mouth water. Her legs were open in welcome to him, and he could feast all his senses on the delights she offered.

Of course she was gorgeous. On top of that, her natural scent of flowers and spice blended with the sweet aroma of the topping, making his head twirl. And now, he would taste her. His tongue began a tentative exploration, working its way through the topping, picking up speed as their mutual excitement grew. She pushed her pussy to his face, letting him know without a doubt that he was pleasuring her, bringing her to new heights of gratification. Lily's hands were holding his head as if she'd never let go. She was whimpering little sounds of a secret language, one the two of them were creating for their exclusive use.

Pete made short work of the whipped topping. Fun as it was to spread it on her and lick it off, he wanted to be eating her—tasting her skin, licking her sexy juices off her plump pink folds. He shivered, realizing the full meaning of their intimate contact. With his tongue, as with his cock and his fingers and, who knows, maybe even his toes, he could enter her—know her in a way only they two shared.

He nibbled lightly at her delicate skin, being so careful not to hurt her, never to hurt her. For a moment, thoughts of how he would be hurting her in the not-too-distant future intruded. He forced them away. For now, all that existed was her pussy and her need for him and his quest to satisfy her. Everything else was banished to some remote part of the universe, like the goods he'd consigned to the Isla del Oso for permanent exile.

Lily seemed to sense his momentary distraction and called him back to his duty to her by arching her hips even higher. Oh yes. With his tongue and teeth and lips fully employed to bring her pleasure, Pete decided to add his eager fingers to the mix. He stroked the sensitive area in the folds between her legs and her mound, eliciting yet more moans from her.

Lily's clit rose high and firm to his tongue and teeth. She thrashed around the bed, giving herself up to his avid attentions. By now Pete's cock was fully engorged and more than ready to seek satisfaction plunged deep in her, but he was determined to focus on her pleasure 'til she reached her climax. Hell, he might just climax himself when he got her to that point.

For now, he delighted in every moment, every movement Lily made, every sound. He'd imprint this time with her in his memory and replay it in his mind every day for the rest of his life. Now Pete reached back and began to stroke her anus, putting gentle pressure on the small puckered hole. Lily seemed to enjoy this as she pressed back against his fingers, inviting him to explore there too. He moistened his index finger by dipping it into the fluids she'd already released and carefully entered her anus while he kept up the barrage of licking and sucking.

She screamed. He removed his finger. "Did I hurt you?" he asked.

"God, no," she panted. "More."

Heaving a sigh of relief, Pete remoistened his finger and put it back. She wiggled against him, evidently working hard to maximize her pleasure, both front and back.

Pete wiggled his finger in her anus, fascinated at this new experience for him. His sensations were rioting as Lily tightened her hold on him and began to move faster, harder.

"Oh, Pete," she called out. "More. There. Like that."

And then she screamed out his name as her cunt pulsed around his lips and tongue in her climax.

When she'd relaxed a bit, Pete asked, "Are you okay?"

"Oh, God," she groaned. "I may never walk again, and he wants to know if I'm okay."

"Huh?" Pete asked looking up, not understanding and afraid he'd done something wrong.

She grabbed him hard and pulled his head back down where she wanted it. "'Okay' does not begin to say how I feel right now," she said, sounding rough and tender all at once. "Pete, I've never felt anything like what I did just now with you. I don't know what word to use to tell you, but 'okay' would be like saying the Atlantic is a small lake."

"Oh," Pete said. Listening to her, feeling her in the warm afterglow of their lovemaking, his cock grew even harder. He began to shift.

She reached out and stroked his erection. "Hmm, it appears Mr. Wonderful got a little hot and bothered there. How about we take him for a ride?"

Pete was nearly speechless. More than anything else in the world, he wanted his cock in her now. But he'd wanted to give her recovery time before expressing his need. That was the thoughtful thing to do, right? But now that she so clearly demonstrated her willingness to get it on immediately, he admitted to himself how much he hadn't wanted to wait.

He swallowed hard and nuzzled her hair. "More than anything in the world... Lily, how do you want it? Me? How do you want me? Did you just call my cock Mr. Wonderful? You want to be on top or on the bottom or..."

"Like this," she said, turning so that her gorgeous butt was facing him. "I want your cock where your finger was. Yes, I called your cock Mr. Wonderful. And no, I'm not going to answer any other questions 'til later."

Pete nearly came hearing those words. Instead, he willed himself to hold on—in just moments he'd be fulfilling a longtime fantasy. He gave one flickering thought to Griselda and all that nonsense in his life before—then focused on Lily.

* * * * *

Lily'd never gone in for butt-fucking before. Of course she'd heard about it, but she'd never had much curiosity in that area. And none of her few previous lovers had ever wanted to try it—at least not with her. But with Pete, whole new possibilities opened up. And she'd been surprised by how arousing she'd found his finger in her anus. Of course she'd found everything stimulating when he had his mouth on her pussy. But she was willing to explore further the new feelings he'd awakened in her. From the expression on his face, she could tell it was something he wanted too. Hell, if he hadn't wanted it, she was sure he'd have said no. But he was the one who'd started her thinking about it by sticking his finger where he had.

Pete was lightly massaging her back, his powerful hands running down to her butt. She could feel his rock-hard cock nudging the back of her thigh, and she wanted him in her. Plain and simple. She wanted to feel him move inside her. Of course, he felt pretty amazing outside her too. She wiggled back against him, enjoying the feel of his cock pressing her tender skin. A fantasy of him leaving his cock print all over her body flashed before her, and she licked her lips.

Faced away from him, she felt like she was in a passive position. All her focus was on her back and on her butt. She was hugging a pillow to her, and then she realized her position wasn't so passive after all. She lowered the pillow and opened her legs, putting it between them, between her labia, wedged against her clit. To her amazement, it didn't take long for a new surge of arousal to begin there. After the way she'd just come, she figured she wouldn't be ready again for a while. It was a night of surprises. She wiggled the pillow into the right position and began to enjoy the sensations it awakened.

But this was nothing to what was going on behind her. Pete was running his moistened fingers up and down her anal crack, introducing Lily to a whole new world of sensation. And then, to her amazement, he tongued her crack, paying special attention to her anus. Any concerns she had about this dissipated in her enjoyment and in Pete's obvious relish of what he was doing, indicated by the bobbing of his cock against her cheek and thigh.

Lily felt aroused and curious. "Tell me if anything I do hurts you," Pete whispered before depositing a huge wet kiss between her cheeks. That felt so good, Lily wriggled her tush closer to Pete's lips—letting him know that so far, all systems were go.

Next Pete slipped his index finger into her moistened anus, and Lily murmured her assent. At first it seemed he wouldn't get far, but then she relaxed and he slipped his finger in further. Then he tentatively slipped in a second. To her surprise, Lily found that it fit. Then Pete withdrew his fingers and placed the head of his cock at the entrance of her anus. Though Lily wanted this, she found herself tensing again.

"I'm just going to move very slowly," Pete whispered. "And any time you want, we'll stop."

"Okay," she said, pressing the pillow tighter against her pussy.

With his penis still hovering against her anus, Pete reached his hand to her pussy. Surprised and pleased to have him touch her, Lily moved the pillow aside. He began to stroke her and she grew even moister. He removed his hand for a moment. "I want to spread your love juice over my cock," he said. "Then I'll put my hand back."

Once his fingers were playing with her labia again, Pete gently began to rub his moistened cock along her crack. "I want to come into you now," he whispered.

"Oh, yes," she said.

He gasped as he entered her and began a slow rocking back and forth, barely pausing in his stroking of her pussy. "Mmm," he murmured, biting the back of her neck. "You are too delicious."

Lily savored the feel of his long legs stretched out behind her, the double stimulation of being stroked in front and pumped in back. She moved against his fingers, which caused him to increase the tempo of his thrusting. Lily could feel Pete's balls lightly striking her inner thighs as he thrust his shaft up her sheath. "How is this for you?" Pete asked hoarsely.

"Interesting," Lily said, for lack of a better word. She found the idea of Pete back there more exciting than the actual sensation—though his heft, his kissing, and his stroking of her pussy were all definite pluses. Despite the seeming detachment of her words, Lily felt the stirrings of a possible come—Pete really had magical fingers, and he knew exactly where to touch her to leave her panting.

"Do you want me to stop doing this?" Pete was practically begging her to tell him to do more, to continue loving her this way, and she knew it.

"Oh, no," she said, giving another little squirm that pulled him tighter into her and drew his fingers to her hot spot. She thrust herself forward to get more of that, and she felt him grow harder, tighter, and faster. Pete whimpered and called out her name. And then he came, moaning with the relief of his climax as he ejaculated in her. Feeling his release, she moaned and came, twitching against his fingers. He hugged her tight and then slowly withdrew his penis from her. He lay spooned behind her, and they both began to doze.

After a short while, he drowsily said, "Thank you."

That got her interest. "Thank you?" she murmured. "Why are you thanking me?"

He kissed the nape of her neck and continued stroking her. "That was one of my fantasies, to love a woman like that."

"It was?" Hearing that she'd helped him fill another fantasy brought Lily a whole new feeling of warmth, of closeness to him. "I'm so glad, Pete. More than I can tell you."

"Even more special than doing it was doing it with you," Pete whispered, holding her closer.

They fell asleep, entwined with her back still to him. But sleep didn't last long that night. Each time one or the other awoke, they began making love—trying out different ways of being together, lost in the wonder of discovering each other.

She never did get a chance to check her lists that night. By the time they got out of bed the next morning, Lily suspected she was well on the way to falling in love with Pete.

Chapter Six

Shortly before the *Bound for Pleasure*, Dominic Laredo's yacht, pulled into its berth on the Isla del Oro, Gwyn Verde untwined herself from her fiancé's sleepy embrace. She gazed longingly at his handsome face, relaxed for once in repose. Except for when he slept, Dominic was a man of perpetual motion and energy. She adored him with every fiber of her being, though sometimes he made her absolutely crazy.

Take their wedding—just one day away now. If she weren't absolutely besotted with him and positive that he was the man for her, she'd be tempted to walk away—make that run away—and just leave him standing at the altar, waiting to exchange vows with a phantom bride. But she could never bring herself to humiliate Dominic like that—and so she was going along with all his plans. Even though this wedding went against everything she'd worked hard to build with him in their six-month-old relationship.

For the two of them, from the first night they'd met, it was all about passion, love, control—and trust. Dominic, being the business genius that he was, had reached his level of success by seizing and maintaining control of every detail of his empire. The second part of his genius was finding the perfect people to manage for him. Though he had total respect for his managers, he never hesitated to pull rank when it suited him. Now Dominic had to learn the difference between his relationship with Gwyn and with his Fantasia Resorts managers. Sometimes the line grew very thin.

From day one (or more like two or three), Gwyn had refused to get swept up by his powerful personality. Once she figured him out, she'd insisted that their relationship was not about one person being in control and the other submitting—or reporting in. It was about sharing their power, trusting each other in how they exercised that power in what went on between and around them.

Not an easy lesson for Dominic to learn. Not when there were hundreds of beautiful, available women who would have been more than willing for him to be their complete lord and master. Gwyn liked to think her insistence on sharing the power was one of the reasons Dominic wanted her with him for more than the one-night stand she'd first expected from him—initially as live-in lover, now wife-to-be.

But sometimes she wondered if maybe she was fooling herself. Maybe it was just her wishful thinking that Dominic really wanted a true partnership—the only kind of relationship she could live in. She'd been feeling pretty good about how they'd been moving in the right direction—until he sprang the wedding on her.

By the time he proposed and put a flawless three-carat diamond on the correct finger of her left hand, he'd also planned the entire wedding himself—down to locale, guests, décor—heck, he'd even hired a designer for her gown! Never mind that all his plans were as flawless as the diamond—of course. She wanted to have a say in planning her own wedding.

Oh, he'd done the proposal right—a scene right out of the perfect chick flick. A balmy night on his yacht. All the roses and romance she could ever have dreamed of. No one could do a romantic setting better than Dominic. And then he'd actually gotten down on his knees. Dominic Laredo, down on his knees before her—while they were both still fully dressed!

"You are the woman of my dreams, Gwyneth Laurette Verde," he'd murmured, his voice husky with longing. "Will you marry me?"

At least he'd put *that* in the form of question—not a *fait accompli*.

Gwyn had thought her heart would burst. She pulled him up off his knees and leapt up into his arms, saying, "Yes, yes, yes!" and kissing him wildly.

After they'd celebrated in the best possible way, he turned to her in the bed and began telling her all the plans he already had in motion for the wedding. *Their* wedding. And, once her head began working, she'd sat up in bed, nearly snarling. Talk about him breaking the mood!

She'd stood up—as dignified as a naked woman could be—thrown the ring at him and walked away. Then she pulled on the first clothes she could find and stomped out of his quarters. Not that she could walk that far on the yacht, but it felt good to make a dramatic exit. Dominic, of course, was right behind her.

"What is it?" he asked, for once sounding clueless.

She whirled on him. "Did it ever occur to you that I might want to have some say in my wedding?"

He looked mildly shocked. "You don't like what I've planned? Tell me what's wrong—and I'll change it."

Duh, she thought. But he was looking at her with those big gray eyes. So maybe he really didn't get it yet. He had, after all, shown himself willing to work with her on their relationship. Rome wasn't built in a day and all that...

"Dominic, everything about the wedding's friggin' perfect."

"So, what's the problem?"

She sighed. "Hello. There are *two* of us getting married, but only *one* of us planned this wedding. You have everything so well-planned already—but what if I'd said no?"

A smile played on his sensuous lips that she wanted to kiss. "Then I would have had a huge party to try to convince you to change your mind."

"Aaarrggghh," Gwyn moaned. If there'd been a wall handy, she'd have knocked her head against it.

Obviously, she needed to do more, make herself clearer to him. She'd try again. "Maybe I don't want such a big, perfect wedding. Or maybe I want to get married in San Diego instead of the Isla del Oro."

"Do you?" he asked.

"You're still not getting the point. Remember, Dominic. Partnership. You and I are *partners* in what we do together? If we decide to role play master and slave, or boss and perfect secretary, that's fine. But that's not how we're going to live our lives. Or, at least, it's not how I intend to live my life."

A light seemed to go on over his head. "I'm sorry," he said softly. Gwyn nearly jumped. Those words are as unaccustomed coming from Dominic's mouth as if they were in Swahili. "Tell me what I can do to make this up to you. But please, take the ring back. Tell me you'll still marry me."

How could she resist? So maybe she'd been a bit too smug about how much progress he'd made. But she knew he was trying. And God knew how much she wanted Dominic. So she said 'yes'. And he assured her he really meant what he said. He'd change anything about the wedding she wanted to. Gwyn kept that in mind as they went forward with his plans.

But she soon had to admit it was hard to come up with changes to suggest when his plans were…perfection. No sense messing with what he had in place. Working with Dominic's designer, she was going to have the wedding gown she'd always dreamed of.

In the books and magazines about weddings she was now consuming, Gwyn read that being engaged could be one of the most stressful times in a couple's life. Now she was discovering the truth of that. One night, after a particularly tense day, they were standing at the guardrail on his yacht. Dominic turned to Gwyn and asked very simply, "What can I do to make this all better, Gwyn?"

At that moment, she was almost tempted to suggest that he walk the gangplank. But she didn't want him gone. She did want him to feel some of her pain. But she wanted to punish him without feeling any more pain herself. What better way to express all that than to spank him. Hard. And she told him exactly that.

"You've been really bad," she said. "And I'm the one who's going to have to teach you a lesson."

He went into his best stiff upper lip mode and said, "Very well. If you insist."

She raised her eyebrows. "Oh, I insist. You've been so bad, I don't even know if spanking is going to teach you enough of a lesson. But we have to start somewhere."

He held his hand out to her. "I'm sorry." This time, he sounded sincere.

"So am I," she said, turning on her heel and starting to walk to his cabin. She turned back to where he was still standing at the rail, watching her. "Follow me," she ordered.

When they got back to Dominic's cabin, she took a fast look at his handsome face, now lowered in a mock-humble pose. She wasn't about to let anything about him sway her thinking, or assuage her anger. Dominic stepped into the cabin behind her.

"Take off your pants, now," she commanded in her crispest voice. She folded her arms in front of her and feasted her eyes as Dominic undid his tight black leather pants and lowered them. He had not worn any underwear that day. She licked her lips as she watched his burgeoning erection pop up and wave at her.

"Sit on the bed and wait," she said, pointing to where she wanted him to be.

"I really am sorry," he said softly.

"Too late for that," she muttered as she crossed to the cabinet where Dominic kept his special implements. She knew exactly what she wanted. The brand new ebony wood hairbrush they'd bought in Paris. Nice hard black wood that would look menacing and solid crashing down on his tight tanned cheeks. Just thinking about it got her clit throbbing with anticipation. She might come just from connecting the brush with his buns, but she sure wasn't going to let him know that. Yet.

She slapped the brush down twice in her left palm and savored its sting. Oh yes, that would definitely do. Gwyn positioned herself in the armless wooden chair and motioned Dominic to arrange himself on her lap, butt side up. He was so tall, he had to scoot his feet under the bed to get reasonably flat. Of course his erection was poking down between Gwyn's legs, getting her instantly wet and ready for him. She squirmed in her chair to keep her moist pussy away from his erection. She knew it would be all over if he came into her. And she was not ready to give up an iota of her fury.

Gwyn also had to resist the impulse to fondle his ass. Cripes, he had the most gorgeous ass she'd ever encountered. Looking at those buns, for the first time in her life she began to understand what turned gay guys on. For now, all she was going to do with those buns was aim the hairbrush at them. Maybe he'd start to get the point. Maybe he'd learn that he really couldn't stay in control of every aspect of their lives together if he wanted there to be any real future for them.

She lifted her right arm as far as it would go and brought the brush down with a bang. Dominic flinched, moving his cock up and down in the vee of her legs, hitting perilously close to her waiting folds. She wiggled back to get out of the cock zone. She'd have him inside her, but not yet.

The second time she brought the brush down with considerably less force. Damn. She wanted him to feel the full force of her fury, and letting up after one or two spanks wasn't going to accomplish much. The third time, the brush crashed down with so much force behind it that Dominic groaned. Gwyn saw the outline of the brush and grinned. That was more like it. He'd felt that one for sure. To her amazement, Dominic's erection was growing bigger and firmer as she continued spanking. If she hit him much longer, he'd probably come on the chair. Hmm. Not her intention.

She managed to bring the brush down on his rear three more times before she couldn't stand it any longer. Gwyn had to have Dominic that instant. His erection was too delicious to waste. She'd have her way with him, then finish discussing her anger.

"Stand now," she said, putting down the brush.

Dominic rose, his cock brushing her moist nether lips as he got to his feet. "Feel better?" he asked.

"No," she barked. She strode to the cabinet and got out her favorite pair of handcuffs, the antique ones they'd used the first time they made love. That time she'd been the one who was cuffed. Now she'd cuff Dominic's hands together and get her own satisfaction while she let him experience powerlessness. They'd been trading roles frequently in their lovemaking as they sought balance in their relationship. Tonight she would be dominant only, for it was clear from his *fait accompli* wedding plans that he needed time knowing what it felt like to be submissive. She'd start with just the handcuffs tonight—maybe progress to more expanded binding later.

"Put out your hands," she commanded, willing herself to remove any tenderness for him from her eyes, voice, and stance.

"What if I don't want to?" Dominic asked.

She narrowed her eyes. "Did you hear anybody ask you what you want?" The question brought back loud and clear the source of her anger. She watched with some satisfaction as Dominic cringed. Good, good, good. Let him start to know how it felt to be totally disregarded.

"No," he said softly. He splayed his legs, which redressed the difference in their heights, and brought his hands down to her level. Even standing in this supposedly abject position, Dominic still maintained his basic arrogance—and Gwyn knew it. Well, she'd take him down a notch. Though he had a dangerous gleam in his eyes, he held out his hands for her in the position of supplication. She cuffed them with probably more vigor than was necessary. Good.

"On the bed," she commanded.

With his head lowered, Dominic walked to the bed and stretched out on his back with his arms extended overhead. His erection bobbed up, just demanding to come into her.

Gwyn wouldn't be able to maintain her tough stance with Dominic spread out before her like an engraved invitation. Though she wanted the satisfaction of a full release, she needed to assuage her anger first. One thing she could count on, Dominic's erection would last. She swallowed hard, then spat out, "Roll over. Now."

Moving with far less grace than usual, Dominic flipped himself over and humped up his rear. Gwyn pushed him down, but quickly realized his cock now lay embedded in the silk-covered mattress. He squirmed to find a good position for his outthrust cock and balls.

After she'd fondled his cheeks, provoking more squirms, Gwyn picked up the hairbrush again. Kneeling by the bed next to him, she was able to finally give his bottom the spanking she wanted to. One smack for each arrangement he'd made by himself. She called each one out as she landed the blows: the food, the guests, the flowers, the music, the photographers, hell, even the videographers. She felt her mood lighten and her clit tighten each time she landed another blow. Two smacks for choosing the date himself, three for the wedding gown designer. By the time she finished, Gwyn was panting hard, her heart hammering, her pussy sopping wet. Dominic's taut cheeks were gratifyingly red.

"Roll back," Gwyn said, putting down the brush.

Dominic complied. "My rear is sore," he complained, though his lips were twitching in what she was sure was an effort to suppress a smile. His cock stood tall, proud, and achingly ready. His cuffed hands were once more in the position she craved over his head.

"You got a beef? Suck it up," she said.

He raised an eyebrow. "That's what I'm hoping you'll do."

"In your dreams." She climbed on him, straddling his belly in preparation for her climb onto his waiting cock.

Dominic snorted. With her eyes, Gwyn dared him to make another comment. He didn't.

She stripped off her clothes then sat herself down onto his taut belly, knees bent behind her, rubbing her wet folds and clit against his tight abs. His cock, full and tight, massaged her cheeks. She reached a hand for his balls and squeezed — harder than she'd intended from the sound of his groan.

Good. Now she knew she had his attention. She lay down on his torso, crushing her breasts against his muscled chest, opening her thighs around his left thigh. She ground her nipples into him, tweaking his nipples with her index fingers and thumbs. Dominic writhed beneath her, his head rolling from side to side. "Be still," she growled. His movements for the most part stopped, though she could feel the throbbing of his cock against her ass.

She wouldn't wait much longer to lower herself onto his waiting cock. But she indulged herself in rhythmic friction, her clit and pussy leaving a trail of dampness across Dominic's thigh. Gwyn reached out with both hands to run her fingers along the firm muscles in Dominic's upper arms. Then she ran her hands down his sides, down to his hipbones.

That was it. She'd waited long enough. Gwyn rose to her hands and knees and slipped back so she could take his cock into her. She circled the head of his cock with her hand and stroked once. Though she longed to take him into her mouth, she wouldn't. Not this time. With her hand firmly around his cock, she maneuvered him to the ideal angle for penetration. Then she allowed for a moment of play at the mouth of her pussy.

Too delicious. The bastard was too delicious. She could not maintain the intensity of her fury when he pleasured her. She was so fucking wet that she swallowed him up in one big gulp.

Dominic's gasp gratified her. At least when they were loving each other, she knew he had moments of relinquishing his iron control.

Still straddling Dominic with her legs, Gwyn sat up hard, driving Dominic deep into her. Her clit quivered with joy at their dance. Gwyn wanted it hard, deep, and slow. When Dominic began to speed up his thrusts, she stopped—and made sure he did too. He moaned, then bit his lip to keep silent. She wanted this to last as long as she wanted it to. She tightened her thighs around him, shifting so she could rub the slick surfaces of her plump pinkness along his rock-hard length. Her orgasm started to build, and Gwyn gave herself up to it—why shouldn't she? She wanted to come twice before Dominic did. With a shiver and a moan, she celebrated her first climax.

Dominic crooked a leg behind her and started to move in a faster rhythm. But Gwyn didn't want him to come yet. She lifted off him. When he looked at her in surprise, she said, "Not yet. I want more." He took a deep breath and kept very still. Gwyn could see his cock, enormous now with need. She reached back and cupped his balls, playing with them. She toyed with the idea of rolling off him for a bit, then rejected that thought. After all, she didn't want to punish herself as well as him. She couldn't help wondering if he noticed, as much as she did, that not a single kiss had been exchanged between them.

Despite her intention to last long enough for Dominic's balls to start turning blue, Gwyn couldn't wait. She'd promised herself a second orgasm, and she wanted to sink her teeth and her clit into it.

"Now," she said, lowering herself back on him. Dominic closed his eyes and moaned. Gwyn rotated her hips, clockwise then counterclockwise. Oh, yeah. Every nerve ending in her pussy was alive and frantic for the movement to completion. They both sped up, heating the sheets and supercharging the air around them with their most intimate friction.

"Gwyn, I'm going to come," Dominic hissed, bucking to hit all her hot spots before he began to spurt his juices inside her.

"Me too," she said, lowering her head to bite his lip—as close as she'd let herself come to kissing him.

"Oh, Christ, Gwyn," he screamed as he began to ejaculate deep inside her.

Gwyn was pulsing her orgasm right along with him, calling out his name despite her intention not to.

Sated, Gwyn flattened herself against Dominic in exhaustion. They lay together for several minutes. She knew she was angry with him, but she could no longer feel the edge that had driven her so strongly before. She never could stay angry at him for long—and he knew it. How would she ever get him to change when he knew he could get to her with his cock?

"How are you doing?" he asked.

Too mellow, but she wouldn't tell him. "Why?"

He nuzzled her neck. "Just want to see how my lady is. Was it good for you? Do you want anything else?"

As if it ever wasn't good for her, even with all the tension between them lately. "Yeah, it was good for me," she said hoarsely.

"Great," he said, flashing his usual smile of self-satisfaction. "For me too, though I'd like to lose the cuffs now, if that's okay with you."

She shrugged. "I suppose the cuffs can come off. But we need to talk."

"You want me to leave the cuffs on while we talk?"

She frowned. That sounded dumb. "No, I'll take them off. But don't run away on me."

Dominic's face took on his innocent look. Gwyn unlocked the cuffs and had a momentary stab of guilt as she watched him rub his wrists. She threw on a T-shirt and panties because she felt too vulnerable while she was naked to put forth her demands. She sat cross-legged on the bed

Dominic remained nude. "Lie down next to me," he said.

She shook her head. "Not until we get some things straight."

"About?" he asked.

"About the alleged wedding," she said. And she'd proceeded to pour forth all her frustration, her anger, her disappointment in him. Dominic, looking shocked at the depth of her feelings, had asked what she wanted. He'd have cancelled all the plans that moment if that had been her demand. And though Gwyn partly wanted that—even if they then proceeded to reinstate all the plans he cancelled—her practical side couldn't allow her to make everyone work that hard.

So she'd remained ambivalent during this happiest time of her life. And now she still wanted something to happen—heck, she wanted to *make* something happen—so she could imprint herself on the process. But she had no clue what.

* * * * *

Now on this day, as they were arriving at the Isla del Oro for their wedding, Dominic looked up at her, flashing his Captain Hook grin that she was such a sucker for. Then he reached out to touch her, and she was a goner. She could never resist him, not for long, and dammit, he knew it.

He pulled her down to him. "How about a quickie before we disembark?" he murmured. She could see his morning erection tenting up the rumpled top sheet.

Maybe a so-called quickie would be the best way to start the day—and improve her mood. Of course nothing about making love with Dominic ever really fell into the category of *quickie*. Pulling her brief white lace nightie over her head, Gwyn lay down next to Dominic and opened her arms.

Her heartbeat sped up at the prospect of what would come next. Much as she loved the elaborate scenarios he constructed around much of their lovemaking, the thrill of near-spontaneous humping took her breath away. Even after all their time together and the pre-wedding stresses, this morning she was hungry for him.

He kissed her long and deep and ran his hands over her body lightly, then paused to spend time on her breasts. Her right nipple budded in his hand as his fingers circled, lightly pinched, and played. Never one to ignore the left nipple, Dominic quickly turned his attention there. But he could play with her boobs later. Right now she wanted him between her legs, in her deepest core as far as he could go. "Enough with the foreplay," she announced, grabbing his cock in her hand. "I thought you said this was going to be a quickie." Dominic moaned against her ear, setting all her nerve endings to major tingle.

She pulled him onto her. Nothing would come between him and her to mar their perfect closeness. She gasped when he jammed his thigh between her legs, letting her ride to her pleasure. She nearly came from the brief connection. Then he moved so the head of his penis came into first contact with her waiting pussy. He thrust in quickly, and she began the dance she'd craved.

God, she was so hot and wet for him, she'd suck his whole cock in so hard, she might start sucking the rest of him in too. Like a fucking, sucking vacuum cleaner. The image made her laugh, which jiggled his cock inside her.

"What's so funny?" he groaned.

"Just pictured sucking you in so hard that all people would see was your feet hanging out of my pussy."

"You wanna suck me?" he asked, pulling out of her the tiniest fraction.

She grabbed his ass. "Later."

"I like that," he said, once again nearly pulling out.

"Stay in me or I'll hurt you," she snarled. She was like a ravenous woman on an all-expense-paid run-and-grab spree at a gourmet grocer's.

"Sounds good to me," Dominic said, thrusting himself in to the hilt.

She tightened her grip. He was running his tongue over the sensitive spot at the back of her neck. Gwyn opened her eyes and caught sight of Dominic's amazing ass on an upward stroke. She ran her left foot down the crack between his cheeks, pulling him closer and eliciting a whimper from somewhere in the pit of his flat belly. He sucked in his breath. She increased the pressure on his anus and enjoyed the feel of him wriggling against her foot as he thrust his cock deeper into her.

Oh, yeah. She opened up wider to him, wider than she'd known she could. He was deep in her, making tiny moves that maximized the divine friction between the velvet skin of his cock and her moist plump pink folds. Her clit was throbbing with ecstasy.

Dominic grew thicker, harder, longer. His breathing became shallower, as did hers. Gwyn clutched him like he was a life raft and she was about to go over the rapids. He stroked her clit one more time and she gasped. Her muscles began to clench his cock in the first move to an orgasm that would rock the yacht, the sea, the earth. She was raking her nails across his back, leaving scratches that would last for days—long into their honeymoon. Later, she'd kiss the length of each. Now she let herself go into a screaming repetition of his name that echoed around the cabin.

When she was at the top of her come, she felt Dominic clench and roar, thrust deeper into her in his own powerful release. He must have pumped a gallon of cum into her as he said her name and twined her hair around his hand.

He collapsed onto her, nuzzling her neck, nibbling, mumbling little incoherent words. She lay next to him, her eyes closed, her frenzy abated, nearly dozing in his arms.

She lost track of time. How long had they been there by the time she pulled out of her post-coital nap? It felt like they were docked, the yacht hardly moving now. Resisting the impulse to trace his profile with her finger, she studied her pirate captain as he slept. Pirate Captain. She'd never forget that Dominic was dressed as Captain Hook, she as Tinkerbell, on the night they met. He'd called it synchronicity. She'd called it random good luck. Gwyn had agreed to sail off with Dominic the next day. In the months since, she'd traveled by sea, land, and air with him. Mostly, it had been an experience beyond her wildest dreams, which was not to say that they didn't sometimes encounter rough waters...and still were. Such as the ones they appeared to be entering with their upcoming wedding. Dominic began to stir.

* * * * *

After his night with Lily, Pete woke up and wished he could turn back time. He wanted to be with her for every possible moment, and he tore himself away from her with the greatest reluctance. One magical night—and he was afraid it would be the only one they'd ever have. And being with Lily would ruin him for any other woman.

They had a quick breakfast together in her cottage. Lily just had coffee in the morning. She made him some toast. They didn't talk much as they both sipped their coffee—just made plans for their workday. Lily invited him back that night. Pete said yes, but he knew it would require a miracle for him to be able to take her up on that invitation. But maybe, maybe something he couldn't even imagine would happen...

After the short walk to Lily's office, he gave her a quick kiss and headed to "his" office. Pete parked himself in front of the computer, then searched the room for a possible hiding place. Laredo was going to arrive at Lily's office in less than an hour. As soon as Laredo saw Pete, the jig would be up. Laredo would realize that Pete was behind his wedding screw-up, and Lily would begin to hate him.

Maybe he should just grab Lily by her luscious hand and run away with her—now, before Laredo arrived. Pete could visualize Lily and him together on a small tropical island, making love on the beach under a starry moonlit sky as palm trees swayed and empty margarita glasses gleamed with beads of moisture.

But Lily was a businesswoman, one who took her professional responsibilities and her career path seriously.

Pete had pretended to trace the transport of the orders as he'd told Lily he would. He'd now be able to produce printouts of data and let Laredo and Lily see in black and white what happened to the goods. The real problem was going to be Laredo. He wouldn't be satisfied just knowing what had happened—he'd want to know the culprit responsible. And then Pete would be toast.

Oh, Pete knew that the initial orders for the food and flowers came from a number of different vendors. This helped complicate the paper trail, the one element in the whole mess that he might be able to finagle to cover his ass. Maybe he'd be able to generate so many number-filled papers that he'd manage to cloud the whole situation under an avalanche of confusing data. Then Pete mentally shook his head. He knew he was clutching at straws.

Lily knocked on the door between the offices and popped her head in. "I have to leave the office now for a bit to check on the progress the local people are making. I want to see for myself how they're managing with the imported workers. Thank goodness no one's pulling any diva acts. I'll check back with you right before Dominic's due to arrive, and you can let me know where you're at with the figures."

Pete went over to her. He couldn't just let her go like that. This might be the last contact they ever had before she began to despise him. "I need a hug," he said, drawing her into his arms, registering the look of happiness and deep satisfaction in her eyes. "Actually, I need way more than a hug," he murmured into her sweet-smelling hair. His groin tightened and he longed to press himself against her.

"Me too," she whispered, pulling away only after she'd pressed herself intimately against him and shuddered. "Duty calls. Deferred gratification and all that. I'll see you later." Her voice dropped into a hoarse whisper. "We'll celebrate our successful outcome together." She kissed him and ran from the room.

"Or drown our sorrows separately," Pete whispered after her. He sat down and began to generate paperwork.

* * * * *

Dominic Laredo frowned. "What do you mean *my* computer support guy is tracking the shipments now to see what went wrong?"

Lily was not used to having to deal with Dominic's displeasure, and she hoped never again to have to experience it. She took a deep calming breath and began to explain the situation in as even a voice as she could muster.

Dominic rose and began to pace, rapidly swallowing up the space around him in his vortex of energy. "First of all, why wasn't I informed immediately when you knew the shipment was gone?"

Lily winced, clearly remembering her phone conversation with Gwyn Verde, but now wondering if Dominic had known what Gwyn asked for. "Ms. Verde made me swear not to contact you yesterday. She said anything that came up could wait 'til today."

"That sounds like something she'd do," Dominic, who didn't look real pleased, muttered. "Secondly, let's review where we are. The goods should have arrived here already. A simple, straightforward transaction that should have been completed before I arrived."

Lily nodded her agreement. "With the computer guy tracing all the movements, we expect to pinpoint exactly where everything is. In the meantime, we've implemented alternative preparations, which are well in progress."

"Right. The a computer guy." Dominic asked. "What computer guy? I didn't send any computer guy here."

"You didn't?" Lily tried to get her mind around Dominic's words. Suddenly the whole affair began to take on a whole new nightmare dimension. But having Pete here was surely part of the solution, not part of the problem—wasn't it?

"No. Who…"

"Thank goodness he came," Lily said. "He's our best shot at getting to the bottom of what's going on."

"I don't like it," Dominic thundered. He whirled on her. "I want *all* the information the computer guy has right *now*. And while we're going through that, I want to know the status of all the preparations. And I want to know how he came to be here."

Before Lily could answer, Gwyn Verde, Dominic's fiancée, entered her office. Looking from Dominic to Lily, she asked, "What's going on?"

"Gwyn, I thought you were going to spend the day at the spa. What are you doing here?" Dominic asked, the softness of his voice taking away the harshness of his question.

Gwyn scowled. "Oh, I had this crazy notion of finding out what's actually happening with *our* wedding."

Lily heard the unhappiness in Gwyn's voice and wondered what else could go wrong in the countdown for the perfect wedding.

Dominic's eyes darkened to an even more menacing shade and he ran a hand through his thick black hair. "Everything's pretty much under control, except for a slight snafu that Lily and I are taking care of."

"Humph," Gwyn said, looking around. "From the looks on your faces, sounds like there's more than a slight snafu." She went over to Dominic and put her hand on his chest with a familiarity and affection that had Lily's mind skittering back to Pete, hard at work in the other office. "Tell me what's going on. I'm in on everything from now on."

Dominic held up both hands in a placating way that Lily did not think came easy to him. "I can deny you nothing." Lily was impressed. Gwyn must be even more fabulous than she'd heard.

Gwyn turned to Lily. "You're my witness. He can deny me nothing. I'm going to hold him to that."

Lilly looked from her boss to his fiancée and tried to squelch the feeling in her gut that she was going down on a rapidly sinking ship. She needed to be proactive—and to avoid taking sides. Rather than committing to either, Lily picked up the phone. "I'm going to buzz the computer guy, tell him to come here with all the data he's generated so far."

* * * * *

Pete looked up from his desk when he heard voices coming from Lily's office. First Laredo's British accent alternated with Lily's husky tones. How could any man who heard her voice resist her? But Pete had little time to dwell on Lily's charms before a third voice, a voice that had meant a lot to him in the not too distant past, added to the mix. Gwyn. Here in the flesh. The reason why he'd begun this crazy project, the woman who'd dumped him. The woman he'd wanted back.

Compared to the effect Lily had on him, Gwyn's voice left him lukewarm—or was lukecold a word?

Possibly the last thing on earth he wanted at this moment of his life was to be discovered. Because once he'd met Lily, all his priorities shifted radically.

Unfortunately, his change in outlook did nothing to alleviate the deep doo-doo he'd landed in—no, the deep doo-doo he'd created.

Taking responsibility. Something new and not altogether comfortable. Actually quite uncomfortable. He could try to tough things out, stay behind the scenes—and hope to avoid Laredo and Gwyn, maybe escape off the island.

Which would leave him where with Lily?

When the phone on the desk buzzed, Pete toyed with asking her to come in for the huge number of printouts he'd managed to generate. He could snow them under with paperwork and an ocean of meaningless figures.

"Payne," Pete said reflexively when he picked up the receiver.

"Could you bring in your paperwork and bring us up to date as to what you've found out?" Lily asked.

For the moment, Pete once again took the coward's way out. "I'm at a critical stage in my research right now," he said. "I'd hate to interrupt the flow."

"Of course," she said, her voice filled with respect that he so didn't deserve. "How about if I pick up what you have so far? Maybe you can come in to my office later to explain…"

Pete knew he was buying at most an hour or so. But he was a desperate man.

Lily was by his side in moments. He could hear Gwyn and Laredo arguing on the other side of the door. No matter what the outcome of his adventure, he was petty and small-minded enough to get a kick out of being a witness to some trouble in paradise. From his admittedly limited experience, he'd have sworn Gwyn did not sound like a happy bride.

Pete couldn't keep his hands off Lily when she retrieved the batch of printouts he'd stacked up on top of the desk. As he hugged her from his seat, Lily bent over and kissed the top of his head.

"I can't wait 'til we can be together later," she murmured. "Of course, the way things are going, that's probably going to be much, much later… Dominic's taking things even worse than I expected. Silly me. I underestimated how he'd react."

"You're so worth waiting for," Pete said. He devoured Lily with his eyes as she carried the papers back to her office. He heard the ensuing silence as Laredo evidently began to read the printouts. Laredo was a computer genius. It wouldn't take him long to realize the figures were meaningless…

* * * * *

Lily had sensed some major tension in Pete when she'd gone to him. While on the one hand it was gratifying that he appeared to be so serious about helping to solve their crisis, on the other hand she couldn't help wondering if his stress had something to do with her. Maybe he was having second thoughts about the way they'd been together? Then she shook her head to clear it. She couldn't let her insecurities cloud the situation—either with the wedding or with her relationship with Pete. Right now, the wedding had to come first. She could just hear Alma reminding her of how often the troubles she imagined were only in her mind.

While Dominic digested numbers, Gwyn conferred with Lily. "Assuming the food and flowers are really lost, are we going to be able to feed three hundred people in any kind of style tomorrow? At this point, the food is far more critical than the flowers, don't you think?"

Lily appreciated being able to talk with Gwyn, who seemed far calmer than Dominic. "Yes. Considering that the Isla del Oro is a tropical paradise known as much for its natural beauty as its fabulous weather, I can't imagine any of your guests will be disappointed in what they see. We're making sure they won't be disappointed in what they eat either."

"Which means we need to concentrate on food. So should we be sending to Puerto Rico for burgers and fries for three hundred?"

Lily laughed at the image of Dominic Laredo's wedding being catered by a burger joint.

The look of horror on Dominic's face as he reacted to Gwyn's suggestion soon had both women nearly rolling with laughter. Though she'd always considered Dominic to be a man with a good sense of humor, Lily realized she'd probably just discovered his limits. Dominic did not appear at all amused.

"It's not written in concrete that we have to get married tomorrow," Gwyn said. "We could postpone the wedding 'til we can make sure our plans are solid."

Dominic made a face as if the two women had suggested they have their guests bring their own box lunches. "The wedding will go on tomorrow," he decreed in majestic tones. "And our guests will enjoy fine gourmet dining—not greasy burgers and fries."

Lily decided she'd better put on her best businesswoman demeanor and get serious. "What have you been able to tell from the printouts?"

Dominic raised his brows. "Amazingly little. I'm not sure exactly what this computer guy is doing—other than generating paper. And if I can't make sense of what's going on here soon, I'm going in there myself—his critical moment be damned." Dominic waved a handful of papers in the direction of the closed door leading to the computers.

At just that moment, Pete burst into Lily's office.

Chapter Seven

"Payne," Laredo thundered, springing to his feet. "What the hell are you doing here?"

"Pete," Gwyn asked at precisely the same moment as her fiancé, "why are you here?"

Lily looked from both of them to Pete—and back again. "I was about to introduce everyone," she said, her voice slightly wobbly, "but it now appears that introductions are not necessary."

Dominic went over to Pete and got into his face. Pete's fight-or-flight instinct kicked in. Pete was positive that Laredo was about to kick his butt, metaphorically or in the flesh. Remembering the fistfight Pete had initiated the last time they'd been in the same room, Pete had no reason to doubt his instinctual sense to put up his dukes.

"Why are you here, Payne? You are not an invited guest, and I did not request on-site computer support. If I had, it certainly would not have been you."

Pete knew he'd reached a pivotal moment in his life. No longer could he rely on his buddies, his fellow "Lost Boys", to help bail him out. Nor could he get by on sheer brainpower. Laredo was easily his match, physically and intellectually. Most of all, though, it no longer felt like dodging his responsibility was the way to go. At this moment he was feeling the full impact of all he'd done, and it wasn't pretty.

"I'm here because I wanted to sabotage your wedding," he said in a calm, clear voice.

The room around him had instantly gone silent. Even the gentle whir of the air conditioning and the hum of the printer from the next room did little to impinge on the monumental silence that greeted Pete's pronouncement.

"You wanted to sabotage my wedding?" Dominic repeated in a low, menacing growl of disbelief. "What the hell does that mean?"

Pete would have given anything not to have to explain himself now — in front of Laredo, Gwyn, and, most especially, Lily. Talk about the shit hitting the fan. But all three of them were looking at him. And Pete could see that, for now at least, Dominic was holding back from attempting to kill him.

"Lily, Gwyn, please sit down. You too, Laredo."

"Don't tell me what to do," Laredo hissed.

Pete exhaled. "It's a long and not very nice story. But I owe it to all of you to tell it, and then Laredo, you can kick my butt the hell off this island and out of my job."

"Damn straight," Laredo muttered, his arms folded in front of him and his eyes smoldering like an active volcano inches from eruption.

"Let him talk, Dominic," Gwyn said softly.

Pete nodded thanks to her, then continued, "I take full responsibility for what I've done. But hear me out first."

Both women were sitting on Lily's couch. Laredo leaned against a corner of Lily's desk.

"Lily," Pete said, "I might as well cut to the chase. Gwyn used to be my girlfriend."

Lily gasped, then muttered two words to herself: San Diego. She shook her head, and scowled at him. She looked as if she wanted to run out of the office. Pete held his hand out to her in a gesture asking her to remain where she was.

When he was sure that Lily wasn't leaving, Pete continued, "Gwyn and Laredo met when she and I attended a costume party on his yacht. I went as Peter Pan. Gwyn was Tinkerbell. As for Laredo, he was Captain Hook. And this time, the pirate won."

Gwyn started to say something, but Pete held up his hand. "My turn to talk now. Everyone else will get a turn later.

"Lily, after Gwyn dumped me, I was angry and felt really betrayed. I vowed to have revenge."

"Revenge," Laredo snarled. "After I kept you on at Fantasia despite your physical attack..."

"It really is my turn to talk now," Pete said, locking eyes with Laredo. "If you'll just let me have my say, we'll all come out the best we can."

"Go on," Laredo said, looking at his Rolex. "You can have my attention for two more minutes before I throw you the hell off the island and out of our lives — the way I should have months ago."

"Let him talk as long as he needs to," Gwyn said, her voice filled with as much steel as Laredo's.

Laredo subsided slightly.

Pete went on. "Please note that I'm saying I *wanted* revenge. In the past tense. It's not what I want now — but it's what I started and now it's run out of my control."

"Sounds like a load of bullshit," Laredo swore.

"What did you do, Pete?" Gwyn asked. She was looking at him with a strange expression in her eyes—one he'd never seen before. Not hatred or even anger, which he might have expected. Not the affection he'd once thought he'd seen in her. He had to admit she'd never looked at him with anything close to the same adoration as she looked at Laredo. He'd have to be deaf, dumb, and blind not to register what was going on between those two. And he understood their chemistry a lot better since being with Lily. But now Gwyn was looking at him with what he'd almost label as admiration.

Unfortunately, he'd have to label the look in Lily's eyes as a combination of confusion and—contempt. Well, he'd have to deal with that later—if he had the opportunity.

"It was just a matter of one small keystroke," Pete said. "When I found out the wedding was being held on the Isla del Oro, it just required one small keystroke to divert the special food and flowers to the Isla del *Oso*—where the shipments are rotting as we speak."

Laredo sprang to full attention. "If we know where the goods are, we can have shipment expedited here. Everything can be here in a matter of hours."

Pete shook his head. "No. The Isla del Oso is a small, uninhabited island off the southern coast of Chile. All that's there is a primitive airport and a crude warehouse with no air conditioning. Most of the goods did not survive the original, longer transport there in top condition. Nothing would be anywhere close to your standards—assuming we could even arrange quick transport, which we probably can't. I had the cargo plane dump the stuff there and take off."

Laredo began pacing. "Payne, you have ten minutes to get your ass off my island—before I have you arrested."

"I understand, boy do I understand, where you're coming from, Laredo. Over the past few days, I've learned a lifetime worth of everything that I've done that was wrong. There's a lot I can't undo, but I'm asking for the chance to try to make it up to you." He looked at Lily, at Gwyn and Dominic, hoping to communicate how sorry he was.

"No way you can make this up to me. Get off this island now." Laredo started heading toward Pete as if he planned to eject him bodily.

Gwyn stood up, got between the two men, put her hand on Laredo's chest, and shook her head. "No, Dominic."

Laredo glared at her. "No?" he asked incredulously. "The guy's a menace."

"That's right, no," Gwyn said. "Look. Pete made this mess, now he's offering to try to make it good. I say we give him that chance."

Glaring, Laredo refolded his arms in front of his chest. "I don't want to give him another chance. I gave him one last time around, and look what happened."

Gwyn made a "what-can-you-do gesture". "I know. But I sense Pete really means what he's saying now."

"I do," he said. Three pairs of eyes turned and glared at him.

"Shut up, Payne, or I'll beat your ass," Laredo hissed.

Gwyn picked up her thread. "Let's make Pete be part of fixing the mess he made. At this point, if I understand correctly, we need all the hands we can get. Then, after we pull a beautiful wedding together, you can beat his ass—if you still want to."

"I'm going to let him stay and work his tail off—but only because you're asking me to," Laredo said to Gwyn. "We've all got work to do." He turned to Pete. "Payne, if you do anything from here on to further screw things up…"

"I won't," Pete said quietly.

As they all left the office, Lily turned to Pete and said the seven words he'd most hoped not to hear: "I never want to see you again."

* * * * *

When they'd separated from Lily and Payne and gone to the small office Dominic maintained on-site, he turned to Gwyn. "Why did you stop me from booting Payne off the island, Gwyn?" His eyes narrowed. "Do you still have some feelings for him after all?"

Gwyn bit her lip, shook her head, and threw up her hands. "You big lug. Are you nuts? Do you seriously think I could still have any special feelings for Peter Payne when I've been with you for all these months, and I'm marrying *you* tomorrow?"

Dominic didn't know exactly what to think. After all, Gwyn had been with Payne before she'd been with him. Maybe seeing the other man had reawakened feelings in her… "We really don't need Payne to help. Lily has a Plan B operational, and we have more than enough workers to pull things off."

Gwyn kissed him. "Dominic, I love you. It's you and always you."

"Then what?"

Gwyn gestured for him to sit very close to her. "You know how unhappy I've been about the wedding plans—I've told you often enough."

He scowled. "I thought we've worked that through. I know I barreled ahead and made plans without consulting you. And I promise I'll never do anything like that again." He lightly traced the figure of a cross over his heart. "Especially not after the way you spanked me." His eyes twinkled at the memory.

"C'mon. Be serious here." She mock punched him in his upper arm.

"Right. Serious." Dominic did his best to look stern.

Gwyn chuckled. "Yeah, serious." She took his hands in hers. "Look, even though we've hashed things out on the rational level, I'm going to admit now I still feel some resentment in my gut. Oh, I wasn't about to say it in front of Pete and Lily, but I'm kind of grateful to him for throwing a monkey wrench into the works."

"Grateful to that son of a..."

"Yeah, in a way. Dominic, I'm one hundred and ten percent loyal to you, so I'd never want to do anything that makes you look bad in public. But I'm grateful to Pete for teaching us both an important lesson. Namely, no one can ever be totally in control. Not even the fabulous Dominic Laredo."

Dominic winced at this. Eerie how well Gwyn could read him. Life with her would never be dull—and she was just what he needed and wanted.

"I think Pete, with his stunt," she continued, "has just given us the best possible wedding gift. Though I'd never admit it to him. And, from the way he's taking responsibility, I think he's finally growing up. I also think he and your manager have something major going between them."

Dominic narrowed his eyes. "Payne probably distracted Tiger, seducing her away from doing her job. I should get rid of them both."

"Dominic, Dominic, Dominic." She growled. "Are you even listening? How'd you ever get so successful? The last thing you want to do is lose talent like Pete and Lily. Heck, after all that's gone on with this wedding—which I actually feel happier about now than at any time since you proposed—they're going to be better and more devoted employees than ever. If you toss them out now, your competitors will grab them up in no time." She snapped her fingers to demonstrate how fast the two of them would find different jobs.

He knew she was right, but he wasn't about to back down completely. "Hmm," he said, "I need to think about this."

"Well, don't think too long," Gwyn said, getting up. "By the way, I told Lily we'd both be available to help cook and decorate."

"For our own wedding?" Dominic protested.

"Trust me on this, it's the best way for us to make it really our own wedding."

Gwyn got up and walked out the door. Dominic followed.

*****

"I cannot believe how dumb I've been," Lily hissed at Pete as he followed her. "From the moment I found out you were in San Diego, I tried to put two and two together. Kept coming up with five. I knew Gwyn Verde was also from San Diego…"

"San Diego's a big place. You'd have to be Sherlock Holmes to put Gwyn and me together from the clue of where I'm from."

Lily pursed her lips. "No, I just would have needed to be awake and alert. San Diego. And your name wasn't on my list." She laughed dryly. "Good thing you didn't try to sell me a bridge."

Pete shook his head. "I guess it's futile for me to say I'm sorry, or to try to explain," he said, now knowing what a drowning man must feel like when a shark fin cuts his rescue line.

Lily kept walking. She whirled on him now and hissed, "I don't want to hear any more of your lies. Oh, you must have had a good hoot, taking me in the way you did. Computer support. Offering me a *massage* in my office, for pity sake. And everything…" Her voice broke.

Pete took her by the shoulders, then released her when she glared venomously at him. "I wasn't lying about what happened between us," he said.

She narrowed her eyes. "And I'm supposed to believe anything you say because—"

He ran his hands down his face. "I know how bad it looks, Lily. From the bottom of my heart, I apologize. And I'm begging." He got down on bended knees and held his hands out beseechingly to her. "Please, just give me ten minutes to explain. And then, if you want, I'll leave you alone forever. But I just want to try to explain."

She looked at her watch. "Not ten minutes, not even one. The only reason I'm tolerating you here any more at all is because Dominic and Gwyn want you to work your butt off to try to undo a fraction of what you did. Personally, I want you out of here. Instead, you're going to stay here. Your assignment is the dirtiest, nastiest job we can possibly have you do. I want you to begin to feel some of my pain."

Pete thought back to yesterday's chicken plucking and wondered what could possibly be worse. But hell, he'd do anything if it would give him the tiniest shot at getting her to look at him the way she had before she learned the truth. "I'm yours to command," he said humbly.

Which is how he found himself peeling and chopping one thousand onions. "Don't they have machines to do this?" he asked the surly sous-chef who, with words of sarcasm cloaked in a heavy French accent, criticized his chopping technique.

"Yes, but they are not to the chef's, how do you say it?—ah—to the chef's specifications. Mademoiselle Tiger has instructed me to tell her if you do the job properly. So far, you are not."

Pete watched again as the chef showed him exactly how the onions were to be chopped. Lucky for Pete the onions were an acceptable excuse for the tears running down his face. He sniffed, wiped his eyes with the sleeve of his T-shirt, and settled in for a long day's work in the hot kitchen.

* * * * *

When Lily caught up with Dominic and Gwyn at her office, the first thing she did was apologize. "He had me completely fooled. Once I saw his company ID, I didn't even check out his story," she admitted ruefully.

"With everything you had going on and his story being so plausible," Gwyn said, "well, it could have happened to anyone."

Lily shook her head. "Dominic, you can have my resignation as soon as the wedding is over. Now if you want it."

He scowled. "I wouldn't think of accepting your resignation. And don't you even think about handing me one. Lily Tiger, you're a highly valued manager. And I predict great things for you in our organization. So stay. I won't hear of any other course of action."

He certainly sounded sincere. "Thank you," she said. "I've certainly learned from this experience. Sorry it's at the expense of your wedding."

"We've all learned a lot," Gwyn said, looking sharply at her fiancé. "And heck, if a wedding can't be a learning experience, it would be pretty...dull. Now tell us where you most need us to work."

Lily smiled ruefully. "Do you prefer food or flowers?"

Dominic and Gwyn looked at each other, then at Lily. "Food," they both said simultaneously.

Lily bit her lip. "The pastry chefs could use some extra hands. There's also a lot of work to be done getting the shellfish ready..."

"Pastry chefs," Gwyn said. "Come on, Dominic. I'll bet you've never in your life baked cookies. Time to expand your repertoire of skills."

"Baking cookies?" Dominic asked, sounding skeptical.

"You'll love it," Gwyn said, leading him off to the bakery.

Which left Lily to help peel and devein several thousand cooked shrimp. After she'd done about sixty, she began to wonder if she'd given Pete the most appropriate task. Was chopping onions worse than peeling and deveining shrimp? A question for the ages.

For a while she soothed her aching ego imagining she was peeling and deveining Pete. How could she have been so stupid, so gullible? Here she prided herself on her wisdom—having an owl as her special animal, for pity's sake. Maybe she should switch to a dumb animal. What animals were known for being dumb? They were probably all too smart for her to identify with. Maybe hyenas. They were supposed to be dumb. She frowned. She didn't particularly like hyenas, wouldn't want to trade in her owl collection for a hyena collection.

She could just hear Aunt Dolores in her mind, telling her a loud "I told you so." After all her hard work, Lily had practically sacrificed her career success to be with Pete. Heck, probably even Grandma Alma wouldn't have advised her to follow her heart so foolishly. Her heart? More like her pussy.

Both. Her heart and her pussy.

Lily wiped away an angry tear. Oh, she'd learned a hard lesson all right. From now on, she'd concentrate on her job—and get her jollies from some battery-operated device she owned and controlled. Her life would be much simpler that way. Never mind that it would also be much emptier. Filling the empty spaces cost too much.

She wiped away another tear with the sleeve of her T-shirt. No one was going to see her cry.

By the time Lily went to bed that night, she personally had peeled and deveined five hundred shrimp and scooped the meat out of three hundred lobster tails. She'd also checked in with each and every chef and florist. The alternate preparations had been carried out flawlessly. All systems were go for Dominic and Gwyn's wedding the next day. Even the weather would be perfect—of course. The festivities would begin in the morning with a champagne breakfast for three hundred. Entertainment—music and dancers and so much more—followed by lunch. More entertainment—magic shows, demonstrations of local crafts, sports in and out of the water, and always the music and dancing—as Dominic and Gwyn circulated to greet each and every guest. The actual ceremony at five o'clock on the beach. Then dinner, dancing, and more entertainment. Dominic and Gwyn would leave for their honeymoon that night.

And then Lily would pick up the pieces and go on with her life.

* * * * *

By the time Pete fell into a narrow, solitary cot that night, he hoped never to see another onion again. But he had managed to peel and chop all one thousand. As his gear was still at Lily's cottage, he'd have to figure out a way retrieve it—tomorrow. For tonight, thank goodness one of the other kitchen slaves had taken pity on him and brought him to the residence. His bed had been assigned to someone else, and the place was full. They'd managed to locate a spare cot and set it up in the hall, and here he was.

Before he'd left the kitchen, Pete received a hand-delivered letter. Now he wiped his onion-saturated fingers on his shorts and, hoping it was a reprieve from Lily, opened it. No word from Lily. To his shock he had an invitation to the wedding—with a personal note from Gwyn asking him to be sure to attend—as a special favor to her.

Having to attend the wedding was like the final lash with Laredo's whip. Well, Pete figured he owed it to Gwyn to suffer through her wedding. Even to Laredo. So he'd be there to see the moment of Laredo's triumph and his own flaming defeat. Though of course he'd long concluded that Gwyn had made the right choice—for all of them. Now his real defeat would look like Lily turning away from him permanently.

Of course, Pete had nothing remotely appropriate to wear to a posh wedding. Maybe he'd be able to borrow reasonable clothes from one of the waiters or… Hell, it wasn't like he actually wanted to go to the wedding. He'd have to be sure to keep out of Lily's way. For several hundred reasons. Though he'd have to talk to her at some point to get his stuff back. His plane tickets and everything else he needed to get back to what was left of his life were in his bag back at her place. But he could just phone her, he supposed, arrange for his things to be left somewhere.

What a difference one night and one day made. Crunching into a fetal position, Pete fell into a restless sleep.

Why was it not a surprise to wake up to a perfect day — at least as far as weather went? Next to his bed, Pete found his duffel bag, laptop, plus a tuxedo in his size, and everything he needed to look normal for the day of wedding festivities. Everything he could want — except Lily.

Since the day's early events were informal, Pete put on shorts and headed out. He couldn't go two steps without seeing some part of the celebration — such a contrast to his dark despair. The wedding was everywhere. As the day went on, he had to give Laredo credit for orchestrating a magnificent event. The man really was a genius. He'd foreseen everything to provide his guests with a never-to-be-forgotten festivity. Buffet champagne breakfasts were served throughout the morning at multiple sites around the island. Guests were then free to watch a soccer game, listen to folk tales, take excursions on glass-bottomed ships, even go in for snorkeling, or arrange for their own entertainment. Diehard shoppers could take shuttles to the island's various shops.

Pete was about to tuck into a plateful of waffles smothered with fresh fruit and whipped cream when he heard a familiar voice. "I thought you weren't coming to the wedding," Victoria Laredo said by way of greeting. "I see you've changed your mind."

Pete shrugged. As he remembered, he didn't have to actually say much to keep a conversation going with her.

Dressed in white linen shorts and a black halter, this morning she looked like a page from a glossy travel magazine. "Just leave it to Dominic to have everything perfect," she said in admiration. "Of course I can't get too caught up in the fun and games today. Gwyn picked me to be one of her bridal attendants, don't you know? Lots of photos and the rehearsal this afternoon. But I intend to have fun, fun, fun 'til the photographers snap us up."

"Sounds great," Pete managed to say before Victoria's husband grabbed her up.

Victoria Laredo was the only person aside from the servers who talked to him all day. Despite the crowds everywhere he looked, Pete felt more alone than he ever had before in his life.

Breakfast gave way to lunch buffets at the serving sites. Once again, guests were free to eat when and where they wanted and partake of any fun and games they chose.

The focal point of the day was to be the wedding ceremony at five o'clock at the resort's beachfront. By the time guests, now changed into formal wear, arrived to see their hosts wed, more than three hundred white wicker chairs were lined up facing the ocean. Pete waited 'til everyone was seated before taking a chair in the last row. Dominic's crew had set up an impressive sound system, which broadcast the gentle music of a string quartet. Pete was surprised that Dominic and Gwyn had chosen such traditional music for such a non-traditional locale, but he shouldn't have been. Nothing should have surprised him about the two of them, not even their graciousness in having him as an invited guest at their wedding. He felt, he guessed, *humble*. Ah hell, he felt like shit. Both for what he'd done and for what had happened with him and Lily.

All the usual wedding people, ushers and maids and whatever, marched out. The men all wore designer tuxedos. The women sparkled in opalescent white with gold trim. Victoria Laredo gave Pete a little wave as she floated by in the processional. Dominic Laredo stood out in front of the assembly, looking about as nervous as he ever looked, with some guy who resembled him, probably one of his brothers, on his left. An older guy dressed in elegant black, who was talking quietly with both men, held an open book. Pete remembered that the governor of the island was going to perform the ceremony.

And then came Gwyn. Pete caught his breath. Gwyn looked like a fairy princess. She took everyone's breath away with her beauty. As Gwyn's father was long gone from her life, she'd picked Ned Smithers, Laredo's chauffeur, to escort her. Her real father couldn't have looked prouder as they walked down the aisle in time to the stately music. Pete's mind skittered back to the night she wore the Tinkerbell outfit and went to the costume party with him — the night she met Laredo. The Tinkerbell outfit had been some cheap thing he'd rented, a huge contrast to her wedding gown, a magical swirl of silk and crystals and beads that must have cost thousands. Hell, her tiara tonight probably had real diamonds instead of rhinestones like the one she'd worn that night. But she tugged at his heartstrings the same way now as she had then, only now it was a remembered feeling more than a fresh one. And remorse. A shitload of remorse.

Pete hadn't treated Gwyn right, and she'd left him for a man who knew far better how to please a woman. And damn it, Pete had thought he'd learned his lesson. But now, after his fiasco with Lily, it was clear he hadn't learned enough. His stupid plan for revenge had backfired on him, breaking his fool heart and ruining any chance he'd ever have with the woman he really wanted.

After the brief but eloquent ceremony, Gwyn and Dominic kissed for the first time as man and wife, and the beach erupted in applause and cheers. Heck, even Pete cheered for them. Maybe what he'd learned from all this was to be a good loser. For there was one thing he knew without doubt this time; he sure was a loser.

The plan for the rest of the evening and night included a very long reception line, a formal dinner, and a long night of revelry. Pete wanted to cut out after he congratulated Gwyn and Dominic in the reception line, but Gwyn squeezed his hand and insisted that he show up for the dinner. He promised her he would. After how really decent she and Laredo were being to him, it was the least he could do.

One thing he had to be grateful for. With so many people around, it was easy to lose himself in the crowd. Even Victoria Laredo and her husband seemed to have disappeared. Pete hadn't spotted Lily all day.

Damn.

* * * * *

The day was going perfectly. Lily couldn't help admiring how well Dominic had organized everything—for the day had the touch of the master stamped all over it. Best of all, her Plan B seemed to have worked amazingly well. Despite the snafu Pete's scheme created, everything went smoothly and impeccably. No guests could have suspected all the behind-the-scenes maneuvering that went into their perfect day. She sighed, wondering if she'd ever be as good as Dominic at taking care of every last detail. Probably not, but there was nothing wrong with setting her goals high.

Thank goodness she'd still been plenty busy all day, taking care of the inevitable last minute needs and a minor crisis here and there. She'd even managed to scare up a tuxedo for Pete, arranged to have his gear delivered to him so he didn't need to return to her place or her presence for anything.

Lily began to relax a bit after the ceremony. Now they only had the dinner for more than three hundred and the night's celebration to get through. And then this long ordeal would finally draw to a close.

Best of all, *he*'d be gone by tonight or early tomorrow. And she'd never have to think about him or see him again. Which still left a last few hours to survive. She wished she could hide. But she still had work to do.

Which was not what Gwyn thought. "I want you to enjoy the reception, act like a guest," Gwyn told her on the reception line. "You've been working far too hard today. I insist that you're off-duty now."

"I can't do that," Lily said. "There are still so many—"

Gwyn shook her head. "You can and you will." She whispered something in Dominic Laredo's ear, and he nodded before turning back to the guest he'd been talking to. "Now I've told Dominic, and he agrees. It's official. As of this minute, you're off-duty. You're our guest at the dinner and the rest of the night. We insist."

Lily graciously acquiesced. Like she had a choice. When both Dominic and his new bride gave an order, she'd have to follow. She'd been planning to stay behind the scenes for the dinner—both for work and personal reasons. Now she'd have to come up with a personal Plan B.

Dinner in the banquet room, magnificently decorated with native flowers, was a gourmet delight featuring the best of the native cuisine—with a Continental touch. No one who didn't know what actually happened could have suspected that the dinner was not exactly as planned. After dinner, Dominic rose to toast his beautiful wife. He welcomed all the guests.

Then he requested a drum roll for a special announcement: "Though I promised Gwyn there'd be no business as usual today..." Loud laughter punctuated his remarks. He grinned, held up his hands for quiet, and continued, "I also promised Gwyn I'd announce one key business decision today. Just one. And everyone, you know this is really special if Gwyn agreed for me to talk about it tonight." A buzz arose from the guests. "First, I need to call two special people up here. Another drum roll, please." The drummer tapped out several notes. "Lily Tiger, please join me here on the dais."

Lily, who'd been drinking some water, nearly choked. What was this about? Dominic wanted her to stand with him in front of everyone? She wanted to crawl away somewhere and hide, but there was no way she could ignore his summons. Standing up and smoothing her black silk gown, she made her way over to him. Dominic took her hand. What the hell? He wasn't about to fire her in front of more than three hundred people, was he? The man would have to be a sadist to grin so broadly if he planned to embarrass her in front of such a crowd. He took her hand. Gwyn winked at her.

"Folks, you all know Lily Tiger as the talented manager of our Isla del Oro resort right here. She's gone over and above the call of duty in bringing our wedding plans to reality. Let's give her a round of applause."

Lily blushed furiously as everyone clapped and cheered. Well, at least he wasn't firing her. For a moment, she could almost believe he was pleased with the way she'd handled everything for the wedding. She sighed with relief and started to walk away.

"Not so fast. I'm not done. Folks, there's a second person I want to introduce. Peter Payne, come join us."

Lily willed herself not to blush harder. After she'd spent the whole day avoiding him, they were going to be standing together with Dominic in front of all the assembled guests. She got goose bumps all over, wondering what the heck was going on.

Pete looked amazing in the tux she'd managed to get for him. Standing between Dominic and Pete, both resplendent in their formal wear, Lily imagined she was the envy of every woman in the room.

"Pete Payne here is one of my computer geniuses from the San Diego office. Without going into too much detail, I'm just going to say Pete has put more time and energy into the wedding plans than just about anyone else except Lily, and of course Gwyn and me. Let's give him a round of applause."

Pete raised his eyebrows, looking stunned. "Now," Dominic continued, "based on the very special work of these two creative and highly talented people, I have a new assignment I want them to take on together." He paused. Lily could swear everyone in the room was holding their breath, just like she was.

"Everyone who knows me knows I'm always looking for ways to grow Fantasia Resorts, new places to expand into. Through the work of Peter Payne, it has come to my attention that there's a wonderful remote island off the coast of Chile, the Isla del Oso." Lily gasped, and Pete furrowed his brow in question. "After doing a little research of my own, I've decided the Isla del Oso might be perfect for guests who really want to get away from it all." He gestured to Lily and Pete. "So, starting tomorrow, I want these two people to fly out there and take on the task of planning Fantasia's next resort. Lily, Pete, enjoy tonight. Then pack your bags so you can head off early tomorrow."

Despite herself, Lily looked at Pete. How could anyone turn Dominic down? Especially when he was handing them the opportunity of a lifetime. Being in on the ground floor for developing the next Fantasia resort. Lily felt her knees wobble. Here she was, poised for developing the next Fantasia resort—with Pete Payne at her side. A complication...

But for now, all she could say was 'yes'. Pete, eyeing her warily, said the same. After the applause died down, Dominic said, "Great! Tonight we celebrate, tomorrow we open the file on the Isla del Oso resort. Lily's fantastic assistant, Carmen Lopez, will step up to manage Isla del Oro." More applause. And how could Lily possibly deny Carmen the chance she'd been working so hard for?

After they'd walked from the dais, together, Lily hissed to Pete, "I expect you to resign. First thing tomorrow morning."

Pete looked at her. "Not on your life. I discovered the Isla del Oso."

"Who do you think you are, Magellan?"

"No, I'm Peter Payne. A man who lo...who cares about you deeply and wants to have one chance to talk."

"I've heard enough of your talk to last me two lifetimes."

Pete scowled. "Then work by my side in uncomfortable silence until you're ready to listen."

"That'll never happen," she hissed.

He scowled. "Then you can always be the one who resigns."

With that, he stalked off.

Chapter Eight

Pete couldn't believe it. In one second, Dominic had transformed his life. Pete saw Gwyn's hand in the magnificent opportunity. But heck, he was grateful to both of them for making him this offer that would kick-start his life in a new direction, one that had been nibbling at the back of his mind. Now he'd be grateful to them forever. And he'd start showing that gratitude by giving his heart and soul to developing the Isla del Oso to be a top-of-the-line Fantasia Resort. Well, whatever was left of his heart and soul after Lily had stomped all over them.

Man, she wouldn't even let him talk to her. You'd think peeling and chopping a thousand onions after his day of plucking chickens would have been penance enough to earn him five minutes of her listening time. You'd think.

Though Dominic had encouraged him and everyone else to enjoy the evening's festivities, Pete couldn't see that there'd be much fun if he couldn't take Lily in his arms and dance with her. Also, Pete wanted to get to work listing some of his ideas for the Isla del Oso. To think he'd called it Never Never Land when he'd diverted the goods there. Well, now he'd be going to Never Never Land and transforming it into a place of promise.

Luckily, he still had his key to the computer room. Pete slipped out of the banquet room and walked to the office. He unlocked the door, sat down, loosened his tie, and logged on. He'd just started his first list when he saw light coming under the door from Lily's office. He frowned. Who could be there now?

Just as he was about to open the door, it opened from the other side. Standing there, elegant in a long black column of silk, her hair piled up in Grecian goddess style, was Lily. "What are you doing here?" he asked at just the same moment she asked him the same question.

"I had some ideas I wanted to write about the Isla del Oso before I forgot them," she said frowning at him. "Why are you in my computer room?"

"The same. I want to get started."

"You're not serious about going through with this, are you?"

He nodded slowly.

"But you've never been interested in the actual running of the resorts," she said.

He shrugged. "Hey, I'm ready for my life to take a new direction. I figure Dominic just handed me a chance for that on the biggest silver platter I'll ever see. You know, grab for the gusto and all that."

She pursed her lips. "I've seen you grab for the gusto," she accused.

"Well hell, lady, I don't recall you complaining. And you were grabbing pretty good too."

She blushed and stood up. "There's no talking to you. I can't even boot you out of my computer room."

He stood up and had to restrain himself from pulling her into his arms. "Lily, you're the one there's no talking to. I'd give anything to have five minutes to talk to you."

Her eyes sparked. "Five minutes?"

"Yeah."

"If I give you five minutes, will you have the good manners to resign from the Isla del Oso project and leave me a clear field?"

He swallowed hard. This was not what he'd foreseen. But then, as he thought about his bleak future without Lily in it, he realized the gamble was worth it. "Deal," he said. "I talk, you listen for five minutes. If at the end of that you want me gone, I'm out of the Isla del Oso and your life."

She sat back down and crossed her arms. "I'm listening."

Pete pulled up a chair across from her. She looked at her watch and set a button. "You have exactly five minutes. Talk."

He took a deep breath.

* * * * *

Lily couldn't believe she was trapped here with Pete. Despite everything, she wanted to just crawl into his arms and pick up where they'd left off after their night together. But her Aunt Dolores self said that would be so wrong. Even Grandma Alma and all Lily's guardian owls would have to admit Pete was a mistake. Lily had a major career move in front of her. She was not about to let her feelings get in the way. So she'd give Pete his promised five minutes. Then she'd toss him out.

Pete looked her straight in the eye as he began speaking. Though she'd have preferred to look away, she met his gaze head on.

"As you now know, Gwyn was my girlfriend. She met Laredo at his costume party, the one I took her to, and she dumped me. I proposed marriage to her, but she stayed with him. Lily, I was so hurt—or my ego was. I figured that she'd just gone with Laredo because of his bucks and power and all that. I conveniently forgot how often she told me she was unhappy with me and all the ways she wanted me to be different. I thought she was being too demanding.

"After she left with Laredo, I wanted to get back at them. I waited 'til the perfect chance came, and you know the results of that. But then some funny things began to happen. On my way to the Isla del Oro, I met a really special lady named Nan in Miami."

Great, now he was going to brag to her about other women. That was all she needed. Still, she had promised him five minutes. Her timer had not yet gone off.

"Nan and I spent some close time together. She thanked me, and she told me something real important. That I had a lot of potential as far as women go, but that potential wasn't yet filled. I began to wonder if maybe Gwyn had had a point. And then I came to the Isla del Oro, and I met the most special lady of my life. You.

"You were like a gift from heaven dropped into my life. I met you with a lie on my lips. And about a thousand times, I wanted to tell you the truth. But I knew you'd hate me if I did. So I chickened out, wanting to have every moment with you I could. And then, when I knew Laredo and Gwyn would be here, I thought maybe I could brazen things out, stay hidden from them. I knew you had a great Plan B going and that the wedding would be all right.

"But in the end, I couldn't sustain the lie. And you were even more devastated than I'd feared. And now I'm devastated too, devastated at the thought of us never being together. Because, lady, I love you with all my heart."

Her timer went off. She rose. "Pretty speech. I'm sure you found your stuff next to your cot. You can catch the ferry to Puerto Rico in the morning."

He shook his head. "That's all you have to say after I tell you I love you?"

"It's been real, Pete. Leave the keys to this room when you go."

He shook his head and looked at her sadly. "I guess being lost is not a condition limited to boys. Have a great life, Lily."

She heard him return to the computer room and shut everything down. He turned off the light and quietly closed the door on his way out.

Only then did she burst into tears.

* * * * *

After the last dance had been danced and they'd said good night to the last guest, Dominic took Gwyn's hand in his and said, "Alone at last. Let's spend the night on the *Bound for Pleasure*. I want to make love to my beautiful wife 'til the tide runs dry."

She kissed him, letting her love for him flow between them. Then, using all her willpower, she said, "Not quite yet, my love."

He looked puzzled and just a bit tired, making him all the more precious to her. "Why not?" Gwyn knew he was not used to being denied anything.

She put her finger to his lips. "I don't know if you saw, but something big is going on between Lily Tiger and Pete. They both left early and looked like they were auditioning for the death scene in 'Romeo and Juliet.'"

Dominic stiffened. "If that Payne is doing anything that hurts Lily, I'll break him into several hundred pieces," he growled.

"No doubt. But I don't think that's called for. Look, Dominic, I'm going to talk to Lily. I have a feeling I can help with whatever's going down with the two of them."

"Come on, Gwyn. We've done more than enough for both of them—especially Payne. If he screws up again..."

"He won't. Trust me on this, my darling Dominic. When I look out for Lily and Pete, I'm also taking care of us. If I can leave them happy, it will be the final magic touch of this extraordinary day."

He studied her for a moment, then said, "Go, magic lady. Work your wonders with Lily, then come back to me. I'll wait for you at my office so I can escort you home. I can't wait to carry you over the threshold and..." He whispered the rest of his plan in her ear, nearly causing her to abandon her talk with Lily. Damn, the man got to her.

"Hold that thought," she said, looking at him with her most seductive leer. "I'll be back as soon as possible."

Though she'd long ago taken off her tiara, veil, and the long, heavy train that had made her feel like a princess when she walked down the aisle to Dominic, Gwyn was acutely conscious of wearing the gown of a lifetime when she went to Lily's cottage. Well, if clothes made the woman, maybe that would help Gwyn get her point across. After seeing the murderous look Lily had fastened on Pete, Gwyn had a feeling Lily was one hardheaded chick.

* * * * *

Lily knew sleep would elude her that night, but she'd gotten into a white cotton nightgown and stretched out on her bed. She'd cried her last tear, she hoped, and was staring at the ceiling when she heard a knock on her door. At first she thought she was hearing things. No one ever came at this hour of the night. When she heard a second knock, she suspected for a moment that Pete was ignoring her directives and coming to her. Actually she hoped…and then squashed that thought.

After a third knock, she admitted she wasn't imagining things and realized that whoever was out there wasn't about to give up. She threw on a short cotton robe and went to see who was there. The last person on earth she expected was Dominic's bride. Startled and confused, she opened the door.

"I'm sorry for disturbing you so late," Gwyn said. "May I come in?"

"Sorry," Lily said in her turn. "Of course, please come in." Then as her mind began to grapple with the reasons why Gwyn was there, she hurriedly asked, "Is something wrong?"

Gwyn smiled, lighting up her whole face. "Not with me. But I suspect there's something major wrong with you. Look, you can just tell me to mind my own business. But I think maybe we should talk."

Hearing the kindness in Gwyn's voice, Lily found more tears and began to weep softly. Maybe if it were earlier in the day and she hadn't been so worn out, she'd have gotten her defenses up. But she was just too raw and sore and needy to turn down any gentleness.

"How about if I make us both some tea?" Gwyn said.

"No, let me," Lily said. "You're still wearing your gown."

"If you'd rather do it yourself, fine. But I'd be happy to if you're not up to it."

Lily was actually glad for the distraction. In no time, she had a kettle boiling and she poured them each chamomile tea. She dimly remembered Grandma Alma telling her chamomile soothed. Katie the kitchen owl looked on benignly.

The both sipped some tea. "It's about you and Pete Payne, isn't it?" Gwyn asked, going right to the point.

Lily pursed her lips and nodded, not trusting herself to speak at this moment.

"Why don't you tell me exactly what's going on?" Gwyn asked.

Lily took a deep breath. With her voice all quavery, she began to tell Gwyn the whole sordid story. Lily surprised herself by getting through it without another round of tears.

Gwyn was nodding. "Once he began to tell you the truth, he really did tell you all of it," she said. She was rotating the empty teacup in her hand, and Lily wondered if she should offer her more to drink. But then Lily forgot her hostess duties as she focused on what Gwyn had to say.

"I'll admit that Dominic swept me off my feet, almost from the first instant when I saw him at that party," Gwyn said. "And though we've had our moments, I haven't regretted anything I've done since I met him—except, maybe, the way I left things with Pete."

Lily's mouth opened in surprise.

"Oh, Dominic's the man for me—and Pete never was. One of my problems with Pete was that I kept trying to change him." She smiled again at Lily. "From what I've seen and heard now, sounds like he's changed in lots of great ways on his own. Peter Payne's grown up—and that's fantastic."

"But he lied to me—about who he was and why he was here," Lily said.

Gwyn nodded. "He played fast and loose with the truth at first, but he eventually took responsibility. And he explained everything to you."

Lily was wringing her hands. "He tried to. I refused to listen."

"And he kept his promise about withdrawing from the Isla del Oso project."

"He did."

"Lily, maybe I'm being presumptuous here. But how do you feel about Pete?"

Now Lily's tears began to flow again. "He's the most special man I've ever met. We're compatible on about a million levels—or at least I thought we were."

"And he cares about you?"

"He said he loves me."

"Pete used the 'L' word with you? Heck, Lily, I thought he was allergic to that word. And all the time he was saving it for the right woman."

"You think that's me?"

Gwyn smiled. "I think you've worked miracles in that man. I'd sure hate for both of you to lose what I see between you."

Lily bit her lip. "Oh, Gwyn, I've ruined everything."

"No, you haven't, Lily. Go to him. Let me help you make it happen."

For the first time that night, Lily could think about the future without tears.

* * * * *

Pete caught the last ferry of the night to Puerto Rico. Once Lily rejected him, he needed to get his ass off the island, pronto. Funny, he'd been on the Isla del Oro for a few days, but it felt like years. He did not relish turning down Dominic Laredo's offer or returning to his home and job in San Diego. Even the thought of getting back to the "Lost Boys" had little appeal. Suddenly he felt rootless and aimless, like a real lost boy—or, finally, a lost man. Maybe it really was time to look for something else, change his life. He didn't see how he'd be able to continue at Fantasia Resorts, Inc. Too many bad memories.

He bought a *Sports Illustrated* and hunkered down in the airport, waiting for a plane to Miami. Maybe he should look Nan up again when he got there? No, they'd had closure. Better to leave that as it had been. On the other hand, he and Lily didn't have any closure. He didn't want closure with her. He wanted the opposite of closure—was that openture? Whatever. He tried to read his magazine and found his mind wandering to places he didn't want it to go.

After a thankfully uneventful flight, he disembarked from the plane in Miami where he'd have a three-hour layover 'til mid-afternoon. Grab some food, something else to read. He was just taking his first sip of a giant Coke when he thought he heard his name on the airport P.A. system. Must have been his imagination. Who'd be paging him here? When he thought he'd heard the fourth request for a Peter Pray to pick up a courtesy phone, he figured he had nothing to lose.

"This is Peter Payne," he said, carefully enunciating his name.

"Please come to the Information counter for United Airlines," a voice crackled.

What the hell. He'd kill some time telling them they'd gotten the wrong guy.

Only they hadn't. Either he was hallucinating or Lily, looking like the goddess of the airport, was waiting at the Information counter.

"Lily?" he asked, almost not believing his eyes.

She turned her dazzling smile on him. "There you are, darling. I was afraid you'd miss our plane."

"Huh?"

"You know, we're flying to the Isla del Oso."

Pete's heart was hammering as if he'd run around the airport seven times. "Lily? Why are you here? What's going on?"

She kissed him — hard. "You have your passport, right?"

He nodded.

"Great. Everything's arranged."

"But how, why?"

"We'll talk on the plane. We're going on one of Dominic's private jets. It's cleared to take off in an hour, so we need to get going."

They needed to switch terminals. Lily held his hand, not saying much. Hell, he was willing to accept being with her under any circumstances.

As soon as they were airborne, Lily said, "I'm so sorry. Pete, I tried so hard not to melt when you were talking last night."

"Looked to me like you'd succeeded. What changed?"

She exhaled and told him about Gwyn's visit.

"Gwyn came and said nice things about me?"

"She said she always regretted the way she'd left you."

"I knew Laredo was a mistake…"

Lily rolled her eyes. "No, he's not. He's the perfect man for her, just like you're the man for me."

"Oh, Lily. Then you forgive me for…"

"I can forgive you. Can you forgive me for being such a hardnose?"

He laughed and touched her nose. "Doesn't feel all that hard to me. But maybe I'd better try touching you in a different way." He leaned over and let his kiss tell her all the ways he forgave her — and loved her.

"Say," he asked when they broke apart for air. "How far do these seats recline?"

"All the way," she said breathlessly, pushing the button that left her practically horizontal next to him.

"Ain't it great flying private? And trust Laredo to have all the amenities on his plane," Pete growled, lowering his seat so they were even. They'd already raised the armrests separating them. Now Pete asked, "Ever joined the Mile-High Club?"

Lily raised an eyebrow. "You mean the people who make it on a plane?"

"That's the club I mean," Pete said, lowering his head to her breasts and just holding her.

"Pete," she said, "we're supposed to be professionals on a business trip together."

"I promise, this is definitely not amateur night here," he moaned, taking her hand and pressing it to his burgeoning erection.

"Mmm," Lily said. "I'm as serious a professional as anybody, but Mama didn't raise any fools. I'm not about to waste that hard-on," she added squeezing. She took his hand and put it on her pussy, already moist with the fluids that would welcome him.

"But we never have given your penis a proper name," Lily said.

Pete was wriggling out of his shorts. "Honey, you can call it anything you want."

"How about Ken?" she asked, busily slipping out of her own shorts. Within moments, each was gloriously naked.

"Ken?" he asked.

"You know? Ken the Cock," she said. She thought for a moment, then winked. "Let's make that Cocky Ken."

"I like that. Short and pithy," he said. "To the point." He was unrolling a condom and getting ready to sheathe his erection. "You know darling, this first time is going to be a slam-bam-thank-you-ma'am," he warned.

"That's just what Pat the Pussy wants for the first time," she whispered. "Figures that'll get her into the Mile-High Club."

"It will. Oh, it definitely will get her in. Ken and Pat," he said, his voice sounding hoarse. "Miss Pat, Ken wants to join your private club."

She opened her legs, clamped him around his butt, and Pete slid right in. She drew her legs more tightly around him and pressed herself to him as if she'd never let go.

Nothing slow or subtle in their need for each other. "Oh, God," she said as he thrust into her, rousing her slick sheath to full life. "Pete," she moaned his name. He was hitting every spot she'd longed for him to touch. "Oh, there," she said, as he stroked her most tender, vulnerable places. Her clit was screaming out *yes, yes, yes*.

Lily inhaled Pete, her senses rioting with his scent and feel surrounding her. A fortuitously timed bit of air turbulence—and she was coming, screaming her joy without giving a damn who or what might hear her. Just as she reached the top of her peak, Pete joined her. Their cries of release mingled as the plane bore them closer to their goal.

Afterward, they lay with their legs entwined. "I hope you don't mind that that was so fast," Pete said.

"That was great," she said, kissing him. "And the next one will be slower. Thank goodness for long flights."

"I'll drink to that," Pete said, making a mock toast. Then he got serious for a moment. "Lily, I told you that when I sent everything to the Isla del Oso, I dubbed it Never Never Land in my mind, meaning that the goods would never ever leave."

"Yes," she said.

"Well, you know Never Never Land was a refuge for Peter Pan, who's one of my special heroes."

"Yes."

"So maybe for us, the Isla del Oso can be our personal Never Never Land. As in we'll never ever doubt each other or hurt each other again."

"Hmm," she said. "I like that. Only I'd rather think of it as Always Always Land. As in, the place that is bringing us together in all ways."

"I'll drink to that, too," he said.

They clinked mock glasses and decided to get some real champagne for their next toast. "But first things first," Lily purred. "I think it's time to renew our membership in the Mile-High Club."

He growled and reached for her.

The End

PHOTO FINISH

Mardi Ballou

Preview

"I should have known there had to be a story there," Alex said, waving his hands in cavalier fashion. "That our Cassandra Harrell, the gal voted most untouchable member of the Bar, couldn't be the notorious K.C. Berrigan of *Invasion of Love Slaves from Planet X* fame." He polished off another piece of bread just as the server arrived with their appetizers.

Cassandra slitted her eyes at him and nearly growled. What did he mean by that comment—untouchable? Who was casting ballots for that vote? She asked him that question in a low, slightly menacing voice, before sampling her foie gras, which was excellent.

Alex was sucking an oyster out of its shell. Nice tongue action, Cassandra thought, feeling a throb in the moist lips of her cunt. Untouchable indeed. She closed her legs tighter and exhaled. How could such a stud muffin be such a jerk?

"Oh, just some of the guys. At one of the Bar meetings. I shouldn't have mentioned it." He had the grace to look slightly uncomfortable.

"What did they mean by *untouchable*?" she snarled.

"Maybe we should let this drop, enjoy our dinner." He flashed her an innocent look, his eyes gleaming in the candlelight.

"You're the one who brought it up. I thought this dinner was all about clearing the air, but it seems to be getting murkier."

He held up his hands in a placating gesture. "Uh, just that you appear to be kind of closed off from, uh, that sort of excitement…"

"Don't even go there," Cassandra said, not at all pleased that he was starting to sound like her sister, using the "E" word. As if she couldn't have all the excitement in the world—once she made partner and took the rest of her life off hold. She didn't need her sister's meddling, or Alex deLuca's patronizing fumbling. And now she was going to show him exactly what she was capable of.

He raised his eyebrows. "Once again I really didn't intend to..." As Cassandra slipped her right foot out of her shoe and put her plan into action, Alex's voice trailed off and his eyes opened wide, nearly crossing. He almost knocked over his glass of wine. *Excellent*, Cassandra thought, feeling good for the first time that night. She'd wriggled her dress up to thigh level and danced her toes up his leg. Thank goodness for the floor length tablecloth, which kept all under-the-table action hidden from prying eyes.

About the author:

Exploring the erotic side of romance keeps Mardi Ballou chained to her computer—and inspires some amazing research. Mardi's a Jersey girl, now living in Northern California with her hero husband—the love of her life—who's also her tech maven and first reader. Her days and nights are filled with books to read and write, chocolate, and the pursuit of romantic dreams. A Scorpio by birth and temperament, Mardi believes in living life with Passion, Intensity, and Lots of Laughs (this last from her moon in Sagittarius). Published in different genres under different names, Mardi is thrilled to be part of the Ellora's Cave Team Romantica.

Email: mardi@mardiballou.com

Website: http://www.mardiballou.com

Mardi welcomes mail from readers. You can write to her c/o Ellora's Cave Publishing at 1337 Commerce Drive, Suite 13, Stow OH 44224.

Also by Mardi Ballou:

Hook Wine & Tinker: *Pantasia*
Photo Finish

Why an electronic book?

We live in the Information Age — an exciting time in the history of human civilization in which technology rules supreme and continues to progress in leaps and bounds every minute of every hour of every day. For a multitude of reasons, more and more avid literary fans are opting to purchase e-books instead of paperbacks. The question to those not yet initiated to the world of electronic reading is simply: *why?*

1. *Price.* An electronic title at Ellora's Cave Publishing runs anywhere from 40-75% less than the cover price of the <u>exact same title</u> in paperback format. Why? Cold mathematics. It is less expensive to publish an e-book than it is to publish a paperback, so the savings are passed along to the consumer.
2. *Space.* Running out of room to house your paperback books? That is one worry you will never have with electronic novels. For a low one-time cost, you can purchase a handheld computer designed specifically for e-reading purposes. Many e-readers are larger than the average handheld, giving you plenty of screen room. Better yet, hundreds of titles can be stored within your new library — a single microchip. (Please note that Ellora's Cave does not endorse any specific brands. You can check our website at www.ellorascave.com for customer

recommendations we make available to new consumers.)

3. *Mobility*. Because your new library now consists of only a microchip, your entire cache of books can be taken with you wherever you go.

4. *Personal preferences are accounted for*. Are the words you are currently reading too small? Too large? Too...**ANNOYING**? Paperback books cannot be modified according to personal preferences, but e-books can.

5. *Innovation*. The way you read a book is not the only advancement the Information Age has gifted the literary community with. There is also the factor of what you can read. Ellora's Cave Publishing will be introducing a new line of interactive titles that are available in e-book format only.

6. *Instant gratification*. Is it the middle of the night and all the bookstores are closed? Are you tired of waiting days—sometimes weeks—for online and offline bookstores to ship the novels you bought? Ellora's Cave Publishing sells instantaneous downloads 24 hours a day, 7 days a week, 365 days a year. Our e-book delivery system is 100% automated, meaning your order is filled as soon as you pay for it.

Those are a few of the top reasons why electronic novels are displacing paperbacks for many an avid reader. As always, Ellora's Cave Publishing welcomes your questions and comments. We invite you to email us at service@ellorascave.com or write to us directly at: 1337 Commerce Drive, Suite 13, Stow OH 44224.

Printed in the United States
25421LVS00004B/1-72